The Curse of the Turtle

The
Curse
of the Turtle

Thomas Albert Roy

Illustrated by Rex Backhaus-Smith

COLLINS ⊕ WORLD

Grateful acknowledgement is made to the Aboriginal
Arts Board of the Australia Council for their help
in the preparation of the manuscript of this book
for publication.

Library of Congress Cataloging in Publication Data
Roy, Thomas Albert.
 The curse of the turtle.
 SUMMARY: After a series of tragedies befall
Jimmy's family, whose home is built on sacred
Aborigine land, he and his friend, Tajurra, realize
the survival of Oonadera depends on reconciliation
between black and white.
 [1. Australian aborigines—Fiction. 2. Australia
—Fiction] I. Title.
PZ7.R8144Cu 1978   [Fic]   78-6413
ISBN 0-529-05502-3

Published by William Collins+World Publishing
Company, New York and Cleveland. First American
edition, 1978.
Originally published in England by The Bodley
Head, 1977.

For Honi Pikau and Maria—
and for Joey, the Aboriginal boy
without whom the legend of Oona
might never have been written

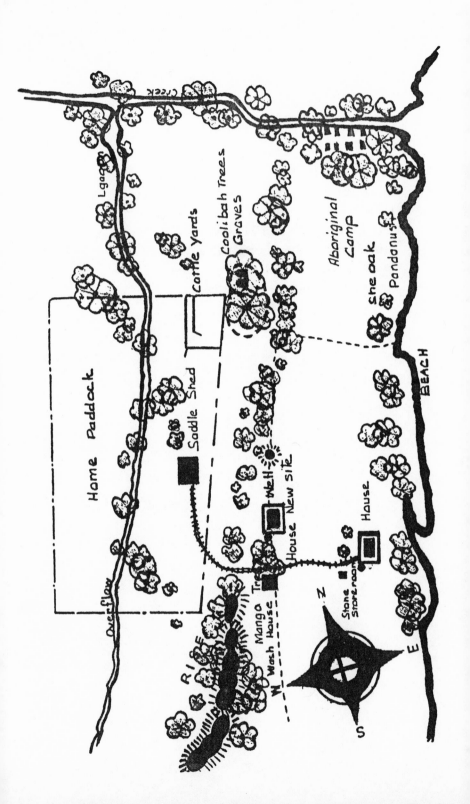

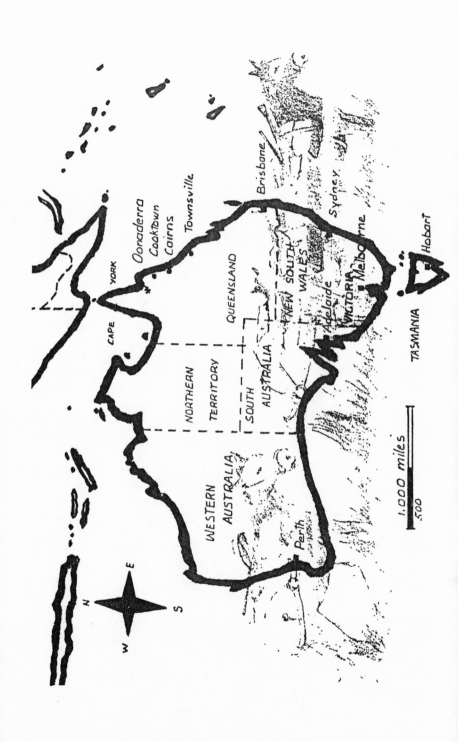

The Curse
of the Turtle

ONE

HERE ON Oonaderra, which was once my father's cattle property and now mine, I grew up almost as wild and as free as the children of Tajalli's tribe.

This land and all the things thereon are mine by right of inheritance, according to the white man's law of legalized usurpation. Morally this land belongs to Tajalli's people, the Oona tribe of Australian Aborigines. They have lived upon and roamed over it since time immemorial. Even the Aboriginal name of the property bears witness to their former tribal ownership: "Oonaderra—land of the turtle."

Throughout the Aboriginal tribes of Cape York Peninsula, no totem was ever more respected and feared than that of Oona—the great turtle. And it was through the foolish actions of my grandparents that the Curse of Oona settled on this property, to brood over white man and black man alike.

As far as I know, neither my parents nor my grandparents were ever aware of the Curse, or if they were, they paid scant heed to it. I first came to hear of it through my friend Tajurra, son of Tajalli, leader of the Oona tribe, and grandson of Tirkalla, who invoked the Curse all those years ago.

The mustering of the cattle from the far parts of the run had been completed, and the yarding of the mob over in the home paddock across the rise from the house, for branding and culling, was finished for the year. The drovers had started out at first light on their overland journey with the culled mob of bullocks to be sold before the Wet set in.

It was a Saturday, and there were no correspondence-school lessons for me that day in the dining room under my mother's firm but loving tuition. I was in the kitchen with her and no doubt making a nuisance of myself. Dad was out at the back of the house loading Nellie the packhorse with sacks of flour, rice, a sugar bag full of corned beef, sugar, and black trade tobacco—the weekly rations for Tajalli and his people in their camp about a quarter of a mile farther up the beach under the pandanus palms where the freshwater creek flows out into the Coral Sea.

My mother called out to my father, "Jack, can't you give this boy something to do?"

"Yes, Mary," he answered. "Come here, Jimmy."

I went out. Dad never talked much. He was a short, lean man, typically the bushman in his khaki pants and gray flannel shirt. He said, "You can take Nellie up to Charley's camp with the rations for his mob. And mind you don't ride her—lead her; she's got enough to carry without carting you, too. Get going."

"OK, Dad."

I led Nellie around the house down to the beach, wondering how Mum had ever joined up with my father. She was his opposite—as blonde as he was dark, and as merry and talkative as he was quiet and taciturn.

And I wondered whether Dad called Tajalli "Charley" because the last two syllables of the name sounded like that. I knew all the Aboriginal names of the children at the camp; they were my only companions. Tajurra, Tajalli's son, was my best friend, about three years older than me.

The camp was a collection of beehive-shaped miamias thatched over with blady grass and pandanus leaves, in which each man and his woman and children slept, guarded from debbil-debbils by a smoldering fire in front of the small opening into each shelter. At the back of these, separated from the main camp, was a long thatched shelter in which the young men slept until they had won for themselves a woman from one of the other tribes with a totem compatible with their own.

When I reached the camp, it was deserted except for old Ninji, up in the middle of the mia-mias, who was squatting naked on the ground by her fire with an empty pipe in her toothless mouth. Straightaway she asked in pidgin English, which was as familiar to me as English itself, "You bring 'bacca?"

"Yes, got it longa pack." I dropped Nellie's halter rope, then unloaded the rations onto the ground. I gave Ninji the block of trade tobacco and watched her prize off one of the pressed, thin black cakes to fill her pipe. While she nicked off pieces with her thumbnail and filled the bowl, I watched her long, flattened breasts flapping against her wrinkled belly. She was no longer interested in me, so I asked, "Where is everybody?"

Before answering, she picked up a live coal from the fire and put it on top of the tobacco in her pipe and stuck the stem in her mouth. After a few puffs she pointed up the beach in the direction of Rocky Point and said, "Some fella go catch 'im fish; other fella go longa trees catch 'im meat." She jerked her thumb over her shoulder to show the direction and then added that the women and children were down at the creek looking for yams.

5

I was disappointed, because I had been looking forward to a game with the camp kids, especially with Tajurra. I told the old woman I was going back home. She nodded and went on sucking at her pipe.

When I had led Nellie out to the beach, an idea struck me: Tajalli's mia-mia was the last one fronting the sea. Curiosity to look inside was too much, although I knew, from what Tajurra had often told me, that the leader's mia-mia was taboo to all except himself and his woman.

Only after initiation are the young men allowed to know of the sacred objects, held in keeping by the leader for the tribal elders, and learn the tribal secrets. An uninitiated boy found looking in the leader's mia-mia would probably be sentenced to death. But that, of course, would not apply to me, a white boy. Anyway, I told myself, how would Tajalli ever know I had been near his mia-mia?

I should have known better.

I tethered Nellie to a pandanus palm, out of sight of old Ninji, and then made my way back to Tajalli's mia-mia. It was only about three paces from the sand's edge over the bare, rock-hard ground on which the mia-mia stood. I crossed over and pushed the bark flap away from the low entrance. The pungent odor of gumwood smoke and tobacco mixed with an acrid human smell wafted out from inside. I crept in and waited a moment or so for my eyes to become accustomed to the dim light.

Then I saw Tajalli's heavy, polished bark shield, which I had never seen before. It was resting against the thatch of the wall; on it, and almost covering it, was painted a white turtle. I looked around. The sweat and dust-stained khaki pants and shirt that Tajalli wore when he was working on the property were piled on the ground, with his blankets and elastic-sided drover's boots beside them.

I moved the shield, and in the thatch behind it was a pair of what looked like thick feather shoes hanging by loops of braided human hair—I had often seen the women braiding hair that had been plucked from their heads. There was also a woven string bag, its mouth closed with a drawn cord from which it hung beside the shoes.

The shoes were fashioned from blood, human-hair string, and thick layers of feathers, but instead of the soles being flat they were rounded and boat-shaped. It was not till later that I learned of the ominous use to which they could be put if, according to tribal law, the occasion warranted it.

My curiosity would not be satisfied until I had opened the woven bag. I did this carefully, without taking it down from the thatch. In it was a carved wooden ceremonial bullroarer with its long cord wound around it. There was also a collection of teji stones and cat's-eye pebbles, an assortment of dried lizards, a bandicott's skull, and a mummified baby turtle no bigger than a penny. I closed the bag, put the shield back in its place, and crept outside. In the distance, from the direction of the open, grassy forest country behind the camp, I heard the barking of the dogs, heralding the return of the hunting party. I quickly put the bark flap back in place and then ran to the back of the camp to meet the hunters.

I saw them coming, half a dozen men and as many boys, all naked except for the men who were wearing woven bark lap-laps. Tajalli, the tallest, was in the lead, his hair tied back from his face with a looped cord. He was carrying a wallaby, and the others were carrying kangaroos and huge goannas over their shoulders. Each man also carried a woomera and a ten-foot-long hunting spear. The woomera is a length of hardwood about eighteen inches long and grooved out along its entire length for holding the shaft of a killing spear, the butt of which rests against a raised stop at one end of the woomera. At its other end is a downward-pointing handle which the Aborigine grasps when making his throw. Thus the woomera adds tremendous force when the spear is launched.

"Hey, there!" I yelled out above the noise of the dogs' barking. "You catch plenty tucker, eh?" Tajalli grinned and said when I fell in step beside him, "We run too much for this meat. Better we kill a bullock, when father belonga you no look, eh?" He roared with laughter at his joke. Suddenly Tajurra appeared at my side, and we walked together into the camp.

The men dropped their kills around the heap of rations ready for the usual distribution later among the tribe. Then Tajurra and I walked along with Tajalli to his mia-mia. Suddenly he stopped and looked at the bare baked ground; then he looked at me, and his face was twitching with suppressed fury. With the amazing ability of his race to read the tiniest of tracks, he had spotted mine immediately, although they were absolutely invisible to me. He said savagely, all the while glaring angrily at me, "You been in mia-mia belonga me." I saw his hand clench in his spear shaft; for a moment I fully expected him to drive the terrible barb into me.

I lied in desperation to save myself: "No, me no look in your place!" I shouted.

Tajurra jumped out of range of his father's wrath and turned to me. "Don't lie, Jimmy; track belonga you speak truth."

I confessed at once and apologized to Tajalli. As I did so, I saw out of the corner of my eye that the women had returned with the pickaninnies and they had their bark coolamons filled with yams, mullee grubs, and yabbies. They were converging with the men of the hunting party behind Tajalli, who had flung back the bark flap of his mia-mia and was taking a swift glance inside. He straightened up and shouted something at Tajurra. The boy grabbed my hand and literally dragged me away down to the beach. Tajalli roared out after us, "Miaja Kadi! Myee Wundul!"

I heard the loud "Wah!" of fear from the people clustered behind Tajalli; but Tajurra dragged me on out of sight to where Nellie was tethered before he would let me go.

Then he said, "What did you do a mad fella thing like that for? Why you look inside mia-mia belonga Tajalli? You always tell me you no look. Now you tell big fella lie; make big fella trouble!"

"I forgot," I answered. "Me big fella sorry now. Why did Tajalli sing out 'Miaja Kadi! Myee Wundul'?"

The words were totally incomprehensible to me, but they terrified Tajurra. His eyes were almost starting out of their sockets; even his black skin could not hide the underlying pallor in his face. His voice dropped to a whisper, and he warned me, "No more you say that, Jimmy. Better you forget it. Suppose debbil-debbil hear you, soon you be dead. Maybe soon you die anyway."

I promised never to say the words again. And I meant it, because by that time I was as scared as Tajurra himself and I dreaded what might happen to him as a consequence of my stupidity. "You get in big fella trouble?" I asked anxiously.

"Maybe," he answered quietly. "Big fella corroboree tonight. Some boys go longa there, get cuts longa chest, longa arms, then go longa big fella fire, no sing out, no cry, no run away: suppose all the boys do that—Tajalli make 'im all men."

He was describing the ceremony of initiating the boys of the tribe into manhood. They were to have their chests and upper arms cicatrized with the tribal marks of identity before facing the supreme test of their manhood in the corroboree ring of fire.

"Better you go home. Tomorrow we meet under tree longa beach," said Tajurra.

"All right," I agreed. I undid Nellie's halter rope and was about to lead her away when I spotted the fishing party coming along the beach back to the camp.

9

One of them yelled out, "You want nice fella fish, Jimmy?"

I waited for them. Tajurra again warned me, "You no tell anybody you know about big fella corroboree tonight, Jimmy."

I gave him my word. He went back into the camp. The fishing party was wading across the creek that runs out onto the beach. Nimapadi, Tajalli's brother, the man who had called to me, was in the lead, the water up to his armpits. He was holding above his head two huge fish—a big trevalli in one hand and an equally big coral trout in the other. He was carrying his three-pronged fishing spear crosswise in his teeth. The other men carried theirs the same way, with the catches of reef fish in their upraised hands. While they continued on into the camp, Nimapadi came up to me and put the big coral trout in my arms; then he took the spear from his mouth and said, "Give your mother this fella fish— him good tucker."

I thanked him. He just laughed and walked away into the camp, leaving me to struggle with the huge fish before I could get it into one of the pack bags and lead Nellie home.

The way my mother prepared that fish for dinner was something to remember, especially since our main standby was always corned beef.

Long after Mum and Dad had gone to bed, I lay in my room listening to the tribesmen with their didgeridus moaning and sobbing out in the open forest at the back of the camp. Across the still night air came the even more insistent sound of other men of the tribe beating time with beeli sticks while the sound of a bullroarer boomed and reverberated relentlessly, letting the camp know a secret ritual was in progress. I got up.

The window of my room faced north in the direction of the camp. I drew the curtains apart. Brilliant moonlight lay over the land and sea. In the distance, to my left, the corroboree fires were blazing orange and gold among the trees behind the camp. Flitting around the fires, like ebony spirits, were several men of the tribe, but too far away for me to make out who they were or what they were doing.

The fear of night and the unknown was strong in me. I wanted to see what was going on over there, but I had never ventured beyond the limits of the house at night except with my father to go riding after some bullock or maybe to hunt wild pigs before dawn. I wondered what the tribesmen would be doing to Tajurra.

And wondering eventually convinced me to go and see for myself. I slipped out of my pajamas into my blue pants and shirt. Carrying my boots in my hand, I got through the window and tiptoed across the veranda and over the rail onto the lawn where I put them on.

Trudy, our dog, was chained around at the other side of the house. If she barked, my father would as likely as not come investigating with a shotgun. But she didn't. I crossed the lawn and set off through the sparse timber for the corroboree ground.

When I was about a hundred yards from the fires, my courage almost deserted me. I stopped. What if Tajalli or the others were to spot me? After the rumpus of the afternoon it was just asking for trouble. But I remembered that the Aborigines would never, for any reason, leave the circle of their fires to venture into the debbil-debbil world of the night beyond. I kept going, moving from one tree to another, until I reached the clearing at the bend of the creek which shielded the corroboree ground from the eyes of the women and children, who were all confined to the camp, some two hundred yards away on my right.

Standing in my line of vision, about ten paces nearer to the fires, was a burnt-out bloodwood tree. I got to it without being seen. One side of the tree was completely gone, leaving the other side with a hole through which I could see, less than thirty paces away, the men of the tribe seated on the ground in a wide

11

semicircle, facing a ring of blazing fires. The men were beating time with beeli sticks, striking first one stick against the other and then the second against the first in a pulsating rhythm of incessant noise. Nimapadi and a much older white-haired man—I had never seen him before—were squatted some distance away to one side of the fires beside a huge mound of green leaves. They were blowing into twelve-foot-long didgeridus to produce their characteristic wailing and booming dirge. Standing in front of them was Tajalli, holding his shield with the sacred turtle on it in one hand and, with the other, swinging around his head from its long cord the carved wooden ceremonial bullroarer, making it boom and vibrate, louder and louder. He was painted from head to foot in white tribal markings, as was Nimapadi and the other man.

Tajalli suddenly jerked the cord, caught the bullroarer in flight, and then dropped it on the ground at his feet. Instantly the noise of the didgeridus and the beeli sticks stopped. Nimapadi and the other man leapt to their feet and ran to face the semicircle of silent tribesmen. For about five minutes the two men addressed them, and then they stepped away to one side as the six men of that day's hunting party, all with white tribal markings, stepped out from among the tribesmen, armed with woomeras and killing spears. Behind each man was one of the boys, including Tajurra, who had taken part in that day's hunt.

The men and boys lined up to face Tajalli, who stood with his shield in his hand and his back to the mound of leaves. The distance between them was no more than fifty feet, with the circle of blazing fires separating the challengers from the challenged. Regardless of his position in the tribe, Tajalli was about to face a ritual punishment ordered by the elders for his laxity in leaving the sacred objects in his mia-mia unguarded against trespassers. His woman, Noolla, should have been there in his absence. I learned this later from Tajurra, also that if Tajalli had shown fear or hesitation then, his fitness to maintain his leadership would have been lost in the eyes of the assembled tribesmen.

One by one, each man in the line fitted the end of his spear shaft into the raised notch of his woomera; he then drew his arm backward with the spear shaft lying along the length of the woomera whose handle he grasped in readiness for the deadly throw.

When all six spears were poised, Tajalli raised his shield before him and shouted, "Oona!"

Immediately the first man in line threw his spear with lightning speed. I saw it flash over the fires directly at Tajalli. He ducked forward, and the spear glanced harmlessly along the skin of his neck and upward and over the mound of leaves.

On the instant, he stood upright and again shouted, "Oona!"

The next man let fly, and once more Tajalli deflected the spear by a swift sideways turn which spun it from his side to bury itself in the heap of leaves.

All six spears he took without a scratch. The last one he let pass between his upper left arm and his chest. The smallest error of judgment then would have killed him. But he laughed, raised his shield above his head, and shouted, "Miaja Kadi! Myee Wundul! Myee Oona!" The men dropped their woomeras.

The semicircle of tribesmen raised their voices in a chant, "Myee Oona! Oona! Oona! Myee Oona! Oona! Oona!"

Tajalli lowered his shield and spoke rapidly to the men and boys. They formed two lines—the men on one side, the boys on the other, both facing the sea. Then the next phase of the corroboree commenced. The men and boys began to mimic the actions of men paddling a dugout canoe across the water. Nimapadi left the other man and ran to the head of the two lines and dropped face-down on the ground. The voices of the tribesmen rose again in the chant for "Oona! Oona! Myee Oona!" while they beat out the rhythm on their beeli sticks.

Nimapadi began to pull himself along the aisle of paddling men and boys in the manner of a turtle. His mimicry was perfect; every movement of his head and neck as well as his arms and legs were exactly that of a slow-swimming turtle. Three times he "swam" down the aisle and back. Then, on a command from Tajalli, he jumped to his feet and beckoned to the other man, who ran forward carrying something shiny in his outstretched hands and stood beside him at the head of the two lines. The chanting and the beating of the beeli sticks stopped.

The men and boys turned to face Tajalli, who came striding across to them with his shield held before him. Nimapadi took the shining object from the other man; as it glinted in the light of the blazing fires, I saw that it was a gold-lip pearl shell as big as a plate.

Tajalli motioned to Nimapadi and the other man. They both stepped forward to face the first boy in the line. The man behind placed his hands on the boy's shoulders, and the man with Nimapadi began to cut into the boy's upper arm with what looked like a long sliver of white quartzite. He worked quickly, making three vertical incisions on both the boy's arms and three on his chest. While the man moved to the next in line, Nimapadi caught some of the boy's blood in the pearl shell. And so they moved on to each boy in turn and in absolute silence.

Finally it was Tajurra's turn at the end of the line. The silence, for me, was almost unbearable.

I watched, horrified, as the man began to make the incisions in Tajurra's arms and chest; each downward cut of the quartzite knife in the flesh of my friend was like having my own body ripped. I wanted to scream out in pain and sympathy, but I held on to myself.

Tajurra's blood was caught with that of the others

14

in the pearl shell. Then the most horrible part of the ceremony began. Tajalli walked to the end of the line and took the pearl shell from the man. Holding his shield in one hand, he held out the shell in the other to Tajurra, who immediately took a mouthful of the mixed blood and swallowed it. One by one, each boy drank from the shell. Then Tajalli handed it back to the man with the quartzite knife, and raising his shield above his head, he shouted, "Miaja Kadi!"

The assembled tribesmen roared back, "Miaja Kadi!"

Suddenly the boys broke away from the men behind them and ran to the circle of blazing fires and leapt across them into the middle. And there they stood while Nimapadi and the others piled the mound of green leaves over the blazing logs until their glowing coals were buried under the mass of leaves. One narrow gap was all that was left for any of the boys who might panic and seek an escape from the heat and the dense pall of white smoke billowing around them in the bright moonlight.

All at once I felt sick and frightened. I wanted to get away from the sight of the ordeal those boys were going through in that terrible circle in the midst of the last rite of their initiation. Somehow I held on, afraid of what might happen if I moved and a stick should break under my feet to alert the silent tribesmen of my presence.

I don't know how long I stood there waiting for what was to happen next, but it seemed an eternity. I couldn't see the boys because of the dense smoke.

When the silence and the waiting became almost unbearable, I heard Tajalli shout out something. Immediately the boys came running through the narrow gap, just as the smoldering leaves caught and exploded into leaping, blazing flames.

On the instant, the tribesmen rose and rushed to

encircle the newly initiated young men with shouting and frenzied acclamations of pride in their performance.

The noise and confusion gave me the opportunity I needed to get away. I raced back to the house and managed to scramble through my window and into bed without my parents knowing what I had been up to. Most important of all, to me, was that I could keep my promise to Tajurra not to tell anybody about that night's corroboree. . . .

Next day was a Sunday, but I still had chores to do around the house, as well as having to make a final check, under my mother's supervision, over my lessons before she sealed them up in readiness for Mort Chandler, our mailman, who was due the following day. I could hardly concentrate, however, on anything. My mind was full of the previous night's events, and I was anxious to meet Tajurra and hear what he had to tell me.

It was afternoon before I could slip away. When I was walking along the beach, I saw Tajurra come running from under the pandanus palms at the front of the camp to meet me. He stopped halfway to wait for me in the shade of a she-oak overhanging the beach.

Tajurra's hair was now tied back from his face with a looped cord, and he was wearing the woven bark lap-lap of a man, just like his father. We greeted each other, and he proudly let me inspect the three verticle incisions on both of his upper arms and the three on his chest. The wounds were filled with a mixture of wood ash and clay so they would heal in the characteristic raised scars of the men of his tribe.

"They hurt you?" I asked.

He shook his head and said, "Sit down. I want tell you big fella story about the debbil-debbil belonga big turtle."

We sat down.

For more than an hour I listened to the story that

16

had been passed on to Tajurra by Tajalli, Nimapadi, and the other men after the initiation.

"Big fella turtle live longa sky," Tajurra said. "Him belonga Dreamtime. Maybe long time ago this fella turtle make all black man, all land, all sea, everything; he bring everything down in the rain. He has given all this fella land." He waved his arm in a circle to take in all my father's cattle property; then he went on, "He tell Oona men, 'All this fella land belonga you; you no let other men live here.' "

"But you let my people live on this fella land," I said.

"No, Jimmy. Father belonga your father took it. He killed the father belonga Tajalli's father; woman get killed, too. All Oona men get mad, make big fella fight with spear, with nulla-nulla. Police come; all Oona men get into too much trouble so they finish the fight, no more trouble. But Oona men no forget."

"We forget that trouble, Tajurra," I said. "So it is better the Oona people forget it, too."

"Oona people no forget—big fella debbil-debbil say no forget, stay longa this place all the time now."

"That is mad fella talk," I said. "Debbil-debbils don't live longa this place."

"It's true all right," he answered. "Debbil-debbils live here long time; they live inside house belonga you. By and by, everybody longa here die."

He was reluctant to say any more about the matter, but I urged that he tell me why. In the end, after I had worn down his resistance, he confided to me the tribal secret he was supposed never to reveal to white people.

When my grandparents, the first of the Brents, arrived in 1895 to settle on the property, my grandfather had clashed with the then reigning leader of the Oonas, Tajalli's grandfather, over the location of the site for a house he wanted to build. Either my grandfather couldn't understand what the leader was arguing about, or, which is more likely, he pigheadedly refused to give him a hearing. It made no difference; the house was built exactly where my grandfather wanted it—right in the center of the Oona tribe's sacred centuries-old Bora Ring. (The Bora Ring is a sacred circle usually enclosing a revered object such as a rock or a group of rocks. The young boys are initiated outside the Bora Ring, and afterward are allowed to step within the circle to have the tribal secrets revealed to them. It is taboo ground to everyone else.)

Naturally the Oonas refused to assist in the desecration of their sacred land, and consequently my grandparents had to pit-saw, haul, and erect every board, beam, and joist in the house themselves. Previously, between them, they had shaped and hauled, by horse and slide, the massive stones that formed the storeroom some fifty feet from the back of the house.

Apparently they were living and working at that time under a state of siege because, according to my grandfather's diary, in which I later checked the facts, both he and my grandmother worked and slept in anticipation of trouble—he with a loaded .45 at his belt and she with a loaded double-barreled shotgun slung over her shoulder while she worked or by her side while she slept.

Trouble, of course, just had to come, and Tajurra recounted to me how it did. My grandparents had been out riding and were on their way home when, over by the lagoon, near where the cattle yards now stand, they came face to face with the tribal leader armed with his hunting spear and with his woman walking beside him. My grandparents stopped, and the leader and his woman stopped; neither party would give way for the other.

From Tajurra's account, my grandfather attempted to ride the man down, but the leader raised his spear to turn the horse aside, and my grandfather in his rage drew his .45 and shot him dead. The woman rushed to the defence of the leader and grabbed the spear from his hand where he lay, but my grandmother shot her down, too.

Tajurra said the shots brought the Oonas running from the camp about a quarter of a mile away. My grandparents galloped hell for leather for the safety of the house, and holed up there to wait for the reprisals their actions would surely bring.

I asked Tajurra what happened after that, and he said, "All Oona men get mad, want kill the white people quick. Old men say no, no more kill'im white people longa Bora Ring. . . ."

He told how the white people were to be lured away from the house and then speared beyond the limits of the Bora Ring. But my grandmother set off to ride to Cooktown before daybreak the next morning to fetch help, leaving my grandfather to guard the house. During the day he could keep watch from inside the half-finished house. By night he slept in the safety of the storeroom, although that was hardly necessary because from sunset to sunrise no Aboriginal would venture beyond the fires of the camp. The Oonas, of course, knew my grandmother had left the property because they had seen the tracks of her horse leading over the rise, across from the house.

For the next three days the tribesmen stood around at the top of the rise, apparently unarmed, but no doubt they had their spears held in their toes and concealed by the grass. They called out repeatedly to try and lure my grandfather away from the house and the confines of the Bora Ring. But my grandfather would not be drawn. Then in the late afternoon of the third day, the Oonas saw smoke signals in the sky to the south sent up by other tribes to warn them that a police party was on its way to Oonaderra.

The tribesmen left the rise, and that night they forgathered with their elders on the corroboree ground to install the dead leader's son as their new leader. At the close of the corroboree, the new leader and two of the elders sat in a circle on the ground. The leader then emptied the contents of a woven string bag (the same one that I had seen the day before in Tajalli's mia-mia) onto the earth in front of himself and the two elders. The teji stones, "cat's-eyes," dried lizards, bandicoot's skull, and the mummified baby turtle had fallen, as Tajurra explained, in a pattern of clearly discernible witchcraft.

Then, Tajurra said, the leader picked up the little turtle and held it aloft while he "sang" the incantation to Oona, the great turtle in the sky, a lay a curse of death upon all Oonaderra by sending debbil-debbils to stay in the house of the white people while it remained within the sacred limits of the ancient Bora Ring.

When I asked Tajurra what the debbil-debbils were, he didn't want to tell me because he was terrified to mention them by name. But I, too, was now frightened and coaxed and threatened to tell my father if he didn't, although Tajurra knew that I would never do a thing like that. In the end he said, "Suppose I tell you, Jimmy, you tell nobody about this fella thing?"

I promised. Then he said, "You want to be brother belonga me, all the time watch out for me, me all the time watch out for you? You want that, Jimmy?"

I agreed. Before I realized what he intended doing, he picked up a small oyster shell lying on the sand and took hold of my arm and rolled up my shirt sleeve. I flinched when I saw he was going to cut me, but I bore the pain of the verticle incision he made in my arm without singing out and showing my weakness. He scooped a few drops of my blood into the shell and some of his own that was still oozing from the wounds on his chest and stirred the mixture with his finger. Then he licked up some of the mixed blood and held the shell out to me. I looked, hesitated for a moment, closed my eyes, and dipped my tongue quickly into the shell and as quickly withdrew it. I gulped and tried to keep my composure.

"We are brothers now," he said. "You Oona man now."

"Sure," I answered. Although my arm was hurting, I tried not to show it, so I asked him again what the debbil-debbils were and what were they doing in the house.

He dropped his voice to a whisper to tell me the debbil-debbils were "Miaja Kadi" and "Myee Wundul"—the spirits of the dead leader and his woman my grandparents had shot. Tajurra said the debbil-debbils had been sent to stay in the house by Oona, the great turtle, to protect the sacred Bora Ring against further defilement by white people while the curse of death lay over all Oonaderra, or until the house was removed beyond the circle of the Bora Ring. He also told me that the area within two hundred yards of the house had become taboo ground for the Oonas, and that is why they would never come beyond a certain point, or Tajurra would never come nearer than the she-oak.

Tajurra said that to prevent further defilement, the debbil-debbils would never allow a white person to die in the house or within the Bora Ring. They would first drive the white people to madness and then to their deaths by violence beyond it. He pointed out that the Curse had already taken the lives of my grandparents, and on the face of it, it had. My grandmother had gone, or been driven, from the house and was killed by snakebite five hundred yards over the rise; and my grandfather had killed himself by walking into his own shotgun trap two miles up the creek.

He went on to say that no white child would ever be born inside the circle of the Bora Ring because the spirits of the Bora Ring never allow any child to be born within it. And he said that a white girl child of my family would not survive long even if she were born away from Oonaderra altogether.

My father was born in Cairns, and so was I. And there was no use in arguing with Tajurra against the fact that we Brents had been on Oonaderra for fifty years, but no daughter had been born to my grand-mother or my mother during that time.

Half scared, half skeptical, I waited until he had finished his account of how the Curse of Oona was destined to remain over all Oonaderra while the house of my people remained where it was. Then I asked him, if the curse of death lay over all Oonaderra would that not also mean the ultimate death of all his own people as well as mine, and all the other living things on the property?

He answered, "True. By and by everybody, everything, die. This place then die altogether—no more white man, no more black man."

I didn't want to believe him, so to convince myself he was wrong, I said, "You talk mad fella talk. Father, mother belonga me won't die. Debbil-debbils stay no more in that house; they go 'way now. Maybe they're dead now. Same like that mad fella what ask Oona, the turtle make big fella trouble longa this place. That old fella leader been dead long time now."

"Him not dead, Jimmy. Him come back."

"Where he been?" I asked in surprise.

"Mission station. Grandmother belonga you bring plenty policemen; policemen catch 'im leader, catch 'im two old men, take away longa mission station. Old fella leader grandfather belonga me. Him help Nimapadi make me man last night."

So that was it! The old man I had seen at the corroboree the night before was Tajurra's grandfather, the dead leader's son from long ago and the man who had originated the Curse away back in 1895. Now, fifty years later, he had returned to his tribe and tribal home-land on Oonaderra.

I asked Tajurra, "What name belonga that old man?"

"Tirkalla."

"Suppose policeman come back, him catch old man, take 'im back longa mission station."

"Policeman no catch old man. Old man die soon."

22

"How you know that?"

"Tajalli no let policeman catch old man again. Old man Tajalli's father. Better old man die near people belonga him. Tajalli make Tirkalla die by and by. You no talk 'bout this fella thing I tell you, Jimmy?" He looked searchingly at me for my answer.

I promised never to tell anybody anything of what he had told me. Then I said, "How will Tajalli make old man die, Tajurra?"

"Give him little drink barata. By and by, barata make him sleep, make him die—no more hurt, Jimmy."

I was shocked, but before I could say anything, he went on to tell me that it was his grandfather who had called the previous night's corroboree to reinvoke the Curse, mainly to rewarn the tribesmen that if the Oona people flouted the taboo by crossing "the line of demarcation," it would have the disastrous effect of bringing about the death of the tribal offender and later the eventual death of all other life that belonged on Oonaderra.

When I pointed out to him that people from other tribes had often in the past visited Oonaderra and had crossed the forbidden area without anything happening, he answered, "Oona no belonga other tribes; him only god belonga Oona people."

I anxiously asked him one more question, "Suppose Oona people go longa that debbil-debbils' ground—everything die quick?"

"No," he answered. "Tirkalla tell me, tell all men longa corroboree: some fella die quick; by and by no more rain come, no more water; grass die, cattle die, horse die, people die—everything die."

Over at the house my mother began ringing the old cowbell for me to hurry home. I jumped up. "Suppose me see you here tomorrow, Tajurra?" I suggested hurriedly. "We go talk longa Tirkalla?"

"All right. You no tell anybody what I tell you about old man come longa this place?"

"No, I no tell anybody. See you longa morning."

I raced back along the beach, holding my hand up under my sleeve to prevent the blood staining it and wondering what on earth the word barata meant.

TWO

THE NEXT DAY was mail day—always an eagerly awaited event on Oonaderra. Our parcel of outgoing
mail, including my correspondence lessons, was ready
on the table on the back veranda. Mum, Dad, and I
were sitting there in the wicker chairs when Mort
Chandler, the mailman, rode up leading his two loaded
packhorses to be greeted by our "Good day, Mort"
while he dismounted and got out our bundle of assorted
letters, magazines, and more lessons for me. He
brought them up onto the veranda. "Here you are,
Missus," he said and gave them to Mum.

"Got time to stay for a cup of tea, Mort?" she
asked.

"Sure, don't mind if I do. Thanks." He sat in the
chair next to Dad. "Saw the drovers with that mob of
cattle of yours, Jack."

"Yes, hope they make it before the Wet sets in."

"Yair—but I don't think we'll get it for awhile yet.
There's not even a hint of rain about."

25

Mum brought tea and scones out, and I passed them around. "How's Cooktown, Mort?" she asked.

"Oh, same old place. Reckon they ought give it back to the blacks and apologize for the state it's in."

And so they talked. Yet my father could never carry on a long conversation; except for a term as a student at school in Brisbane, he had lived the greater part of his life here on Oonaderra. Like so many Australian bushmen, he knew plenty but spoke little.

Mum was quite different; she would have gone on talking all day, except that she was dying to read the latest batch of women's magazines as well as the letters that had arrived from the "Outside."

Mort stayed about half an hour and then packed our mail and mounted. "Well," he said, "I might not be seeing you again for the next couple of months if the Wet sets in on time, so hooray till next time."

"Hooray, Mort," we called out, and watched him ride on out of sight over the rise.

Dad said to my mother, "How's Jimmy making out with his lessons, Mary?"

"Oh, he's ahead of them now, Jack."

"Well, how about giving him the rest of the day off? I want him to ride over to the lagoon with a block of rock salt for the stock."

"All right, then. I was hoping to have a bit of time to myself, in any case, to go through the mail and have a glance through the magazines."

"OK, Jimmy," Dad said, "on your way, and mind you put the salt in that trough under the paperbarks; don't just dump it on the ground."

"Gee, thanks, Dad, I won't."

With a slice of bread for Creamy, my Arab pony, I made off over the rise to the home paddock at the other side, to get my saddle and bridle from the shed and a hunk of rock salt which I put in a sugar bag. I had only to whistle twice for the pony to come galloping across the paddock for the bread and for me to slip the bridle and saddle on him. As I hopped up with the bag in my hand, Tajurra came running across from the camp.

"Where you go?" he asked.

"Take salt longa cattle lick, longa lagoon. You want come?"

"All right." He jumped up behind me, and I passed the bag of salt to him and dug my heels into Creamy's flanks. While we cantered the half mile over to the lagoon, just past the cattle yards, Tajurra told me that three of the Oona men were there hunting wild duck.

The three men were sitting under the paperbark trees when we rode up and dismounted. They put their fingers to their lips for us to keep quiet. We tethered the pony in the shade, then put the hunk of salt in the wooden trough, and squatted down beside the men to watch the proceedings.

Each man had fashioned a long hollow reed from the tall swamp grass growing around the water's edge. They were watching the sky over to the west. Suddenly they got up and ran down into the water, and putting the hollow reeds into their mouths, they waded out till the water was up to their waists, and then they bobbed under out of sight, the hollow reeds, their breathing tubes, just showing above the surface.

Tajurra nudged me, and I almost shouted out with pain—he had nudged the cut in my arm which I had bandaged under my sleeve. He whispered, "Duck come."

The birds were circling above the paperbarks and coming down to rest on the water around the three breathing tubes. Then, one by one, they began to disappear as the men pulled them under by their feet.

The rest of the flock was apparently completely unaware of the danger until the three men rose out of the water near the bank and stepped onto dry ground. In a whirring, quacking mass, the ducks lifted in a feathered cloud and flew off.

Each man had half-a-dozen flapping ducks clutched in his hand. I watched them kill the birds by holding their beaks and biting them behind the head. The whole business had taken no more than ten or fifteen minutes.

The men came over to us, and Alitjira, one of them, said, "Good fella tuckers. You take this fat one."

He handed me one of the ducks with the blood from the bite running down its bill.

I thanked him and stuffed it into the sugar bag, then tied it to the pommel of the saddle. The men picked up their spears from where they lay on the ground and set off around the lagoon looking for more game.

In a way I hated having the duck because I would be given the job of plucking and cleaning it. The later I got back, the less likelihood there would be for me to do the job. Then Tajurra said, "Tajalli no more mad with you now. Maybe him tell you plenty thing about Oona people. You no tell white people nothing."

"I give my word longa you last time," I said. "No more speak about Oona man longa my people, longa nobody."

"You come longa camp all the time now," he said, satisfied that he could trust me. "You want come longa me, speak longa grandfather belonga me? Him stay in mia-mia belonga Ninji."

"All right," I said.

We rode over to the camp and left the pony hitched to a sapling on the outskirts under the trees, while we made our way to Ninji's mia-mia. She was kneeling at her fire, kneading a ball of dough on a slab of bark. The white-haired old man, Tajurra's grandfather, was sitting crosslegged near the low opening to the mia-mia smoking his pipe.

Tajurra said to him, "Jimmy, white fella boy want talk longa you, him all the same as brother belonga me."

To my astonishment, the old man answered in

excellent English, "Sit down, Jimmy and you, too, Tajurra."

We sat down. Old Ninji went on with her work of putting the johnnycake into the ashes and covering it with live coals. Men, women, and children were working or wandering round the mia-mias. A group of kids was standing some distance away, giggling and talking, while they watched us.

Ninji put a battered, black billy on the fire to boil. Then she said to the old man, "Give it pipe."

He took it out of his mouth and handed it across to her. Looking at me, he said, "You watched the corroboree the other night, Jimmy, didn't you?"

The unexpected question flabbergasted me. "How do you know I did?"

"You left your tracks where you stood behind the burnt tree. I saw them yesterday. Were you there all the time?"

"No. I only saw Tajurra and the other boys being made into men. I went home before the corroboree finished."

"You didn't see the beginning?"

"No."

Tajurra looked quickly at me and then at the old man to explain my conduct. "Jimmy no tell about corroboree," he said. "Him tell nothing about Oona man. Him speak truth. Him all the same as Oona man; Tajalli all the same father belonga Jimmy."

Apparently the old man accepted me on Tajurra's word because he laughed and said, "That makes me your grandfather, too, Jimmy. That makes it easy for me to talk to you. What is it you want to talk to me about?"

I had not wanted to talk about anything; I had just wanted to see the old man who Tajurra had told me had escaped from the mission station to come home to his people. So I said the first thing that came to my mind, "Why did the police take you away and put you in a mission station?"

"Because I tried to kill your grandfather and your grandmother after they shot my mother and father a long, long time ago. My parents tried to stop the white people from building their house in our Bora Ring. Then the police came and caught me and two of the old men of my tribe."

"What did they do to you?"

"They fastened our necks to a long chain and dragged us behind their horses all the way to Cooktown. Look . . ." He ran his finger round his throat to show me the deep scar the chain had left, and then he went on. "They gave us no water, no rest, nothing. And when we reached the police station in Cooktown, we were chained to a post in the yard and left there for three days and three nights. They wouldn't put us in a cell because they said we stank. To white people we do, in our wild state; and white people smell to us, too. Well, on the second day the two old men with me died . . ."

He paused to watch the old Ninji shaking a mixture of tea and sugar out of a cocoa tin into the boiling billy. She lifted it from the fire and then pulled the johnnycake out of the coals with a stick and began breaking it up on the slab of bark.

She handed round a piece each.

While we gingerly bit off pieces and chewed with our mouths open to cool the burning-hot cake, the old man went on.

"The police said I was too much a myall black; I needed to learn the ways of the white man; they took me away to a mission station for the mission people to convert to Christianity. They didn't, but they taught me to speak like white people. And I learned to be cunning like white people and not to speak the truth if it would get me into trouble. Always I wanted to escape. I tried plenty of times, but I was always caught and severely punished. After many years I was taken away to Palm Island. That place made me hate white people all the more. I was never allowed off the island. I was thrown into the punishment cells many times for trying to escape, before I succeeded, with the help of friends, in getting back to the mainland."

"How did you do it?" I asked, swallowing a mouthful of the johnnycake.

He avoided telling me how he had escaped and just said, "I was not going to die in that place in a prison cell. I had to come to my people before it was too late. I wanted to be with them when I spoke to our god, Oona, the great turtle in the sky, because soon I am going to die and then he will take me back to the Dreamtime forever."

"Have you spoken to your god yet?"

"Yes, on the night of the corroboree, before you stood behind the tree to watch."

Ninji passed the billy around for us to sip at the hot sweet tea. I asked Tajurra if it was all right for me to speak about the Curse of Oona. He nodded. I said to the old man, "Do you believe there is a curse on Oonaderra?"

Without hesitation he said, "Yes. It was I who made the Curse long, long ago."

"But can't you take it off now?" I asked. "Wouldn't it be better to forget it now?"

"No," he said emphatically; "the Curse will stay all over this land till everything on it is dead. Only your people can take it off. If they take their house away from our Bora Ring, everything will be all right again."

"But my father will never do that. Why should he? He didn't cause the trouble."

"No, Jimmy, he didn't," the old man answered. "But he lives in that house."

"Well, so does my mother, and so do I," I argued. "And what about your people—can't they go and live in some other place away from Oonaderra?"

"They can't do that, Jimmy," he explained. "They have to live here—this is their tribal land. They cannot stay on the land that belongs to other tribes."

A thought flashed through my mind: if only the house would burn down. And just as quickly another thought took its place: nothing serious had happened on Oonaderra in my lifetime; my mother and father were all right, and so was I. As far as I was concerned, the Curse, if there really was such a thing on Oonaderra, had happened too long ago to be worth worrying about. I said, "I'm not afraid of the Curse. It can't hurt me because it hasn't hurt my mother and father. I think it's all over and done with now."

The old man just said quietly, "After I'm dead, Jimmy, wait and see—after I'm dead."

I wasn't convinced, but I had noticed the old man had looked at the sky, away to the south, several times as though he were watching for something. Tajurra had been doing the same.

When we left Tirkalla and Ninji, and walked over to the pony, I said to Tajurra, "Why do you look longa sky?"

"Watch for other man longa another tribe make smoke talk; tell Oona people police come."

"Why do the police come? No more trouble longa this place now."

"Him come all right, Jimmy; catch Tirkalla, take 'im back longa mission station. Black tracker soon find track belonga old man."

I jumped into the saddle and was about to canter away when a commotion broke out among a group of the Oona people on the beach in front of the camp.

Tajurra hopped up behind me, and we galloped down there to see what was going on. We couldn't see anything for the pandanus palms until we dismounted and made our way through the people to the water's edge. There we saw Nimapadi about sixty yards out in a bark canoe. He was belting at something in the water with his long hunting spear. I saw the swift glint of a shark's fin cutting the surface of the water as it circled and repeatedly attacked a dugong carcass tied to the frail canoe.

Tajurra said, "Nimapadi catch dugong, shark smell blood, get mad longa meat."

The canoe was lurching and bobbing crazily about under the efforts of Nimapadi beating off the huge shark, which was lunging ferociously at the carcass. I fully expected Nimapadi to be knocked into the churning water and himself fall victim to the man-eater.

Tajalli came running down to the water's edge, carrying a skinning knife in his teeth. He plunged through the first line of breakers, disappeared, and then reappeared farther out. Three times he dived to swim out underwater. At the third dive he did not surface for what must have been two minutes or more.

Then Nimapadi dived overboard with his spear. The canoe began to heave out of the water and finally overturned, snapping the rope tied to the dugong. First the head of one man and then the other surfaced for air and disappeared to continue the battle underwater.

Suddenly Tajalli surfaced alone, the knife ready in his upraised hand. The fin of the sharp came slicing through the water as it circled to attack. Then Nimapadi surfaced, almost directly in its path. He lunged with his spear and spun the monster toward Tajalli, who was treading water, his hand still raised in readiness with the knife. The blade flashed as he drove it down in one lightning blow. The water heaved, boiled, and both men disappeared under the foam churned up by the shark in its dying convulsions before it sank.

Tajalli was shouting for the others on the beach to come and help drag the carcasses ashore.

The men and boys raced out in a long line through the breakers until the leader reached the scene and seized hold of Nimapadi's hand. Then the men and boys joined hands in a chain to pull in Nimapadi, who was holding on to the dugong, and Tajalli, who was

33

holding on to its tail with one hand and on to the shark's gills with the other; he had the knife between his teeth. The chain of men and boys pulled and heaved until they had the dugong and the shark, a gray nurse about eighteen feet long, dragged up on the beach.

While Tajalli began slitting open the dugong's belly, I took a look at the shark. It had been killed with one blow from the knife—exactly where the head and body joined.

The noise of the camp dogs' barking, the shouting, and the laughter was deafening.

Already the women and girls were fetching their bark coolamons for the carrying away and distribution of the meat when it was carved up.

As the reigning leader of the Oonas, Tajalli had the prerogative of disemboweling the carcasses and selecting the best of the entrails for himself and his woman. He slit open the belly of the dugong and cut into its stomach to let the contents of sea grass and seaweed spill out on the sand. Then he cut out the heart and liver; they were the delicacies reserved only for a leader and his woman. A young girl stepped forward with her coolamon. He put the heart and liver in it and told her to take them to Tirkalla and Ninji.

The men were standing around, waiting to carve up the carcasses. Tajalli turned to the shark to continue the process of disembowelment. I was amazed at what was in that shark's stomach. There was part of a Japanese fishing net with a big yellow glass float still attached to it, as well as hunks of flesh it had torn from the dugong. There was a fisherman's rubber knee-length boot, a half-digested crocodile's foot, and a dozen or more big kingfish and tuna.

Tajalli then cut portions from the shark's heart and its huge liver. Noola, his woman, came forward with her coolamon and took the portions and carried them away to his mia-mia.

Tajalli stepped back from the carcasses. His cere-

34

monial right to be the first to carve and take his portions of shark or dugong was over.

The other men swarmed over the bodies to cut and hack them up for distribution.

Tajurra, who was standing beside me, said, "Father come, Jimmy."

I looked around. Dad in his familiar khaki pants, wide-brimmed Stetson hat, and gray shirt was riding toward us from across the rise on his favorite horse, the big chestnut. Trudy, his blue cattle dog, was trotting behind.

I left Tajurra and hopped up into the saddle of Creamy. Dad rode up to me, his Stetson pushed back from his lean dark face. He said, "Weren't you supposed to go over to the lagoon with that rock salt I told you to take?"

I said, "I have, Dad. Got a duck, too, from one of the men over there." I patted the bag on the pommel.

He glanced at the bag and shouted to Tajalli, "Hey, you! Charley! Come here!"

"Yes, Boss," Tajalli answered and came over to us.

At that moment I hated my father for his arrogance. I thought, What right has he to treat Tajalli like a child, in front of the whole tribe? To him, the Aborigines were either "boongs, burries" or "blacks," or he called them by ridiculous nicknames, such as "Charley" for Tajalli, "Paddy" for Nimapadi, and so on. The women were "gins, lubras" or "Marys," or given equally stupid nicknames such as "Lizzie" or "Bella."

Dad said to Tajalli, "Missus want two fella Mary come longa washhouse, wash clothes in the morning."

"Yes, Boss. Me send two fella woman longa Missus."

"And me want four, five men come longa me get plenty firewood, Charley. You send 'im longa home paddock, longa morning. OK?"

"Yes, Boss. Me send men longa morning."

"You come too, Charley?"

"Maybe, Boss, maybe."

"All right, Charley, you can clear out now."

Tajalli walked back to his people on the beach.

Dad swung the chestnut round and said, "Come on, Jimmy. If we're going to get that duck cleaned, we'd better let the horses go and get started on it."

I rode behind him in silence across the rise and over to the saddle shed. We let the horses go and carried our saddles and bridles into the shed. I put the duck on the big table near the doorway. While we were hanging up the bridles and putting the saddles on the two long rails at the other end of the shed, Dad broke his silence to say, "I want to have a bit of a talk with you, Jimmy."

"Yes, Dad."

We came back to the big table and sat on its edge.

"Got news for you," he began. "Mum and I got a letter in the mail from the Church of England Grammar School in Brisbane. It's all been fixed for you to go down there as a boarder."

My heart sank. I had known that my parents had been seeking to enroll me as a boarder at the school, but now that it was confirmed, I dreaded having to leave Oonaderra. I was thirteen, almost fourteen, and had never left the property except for a couple of trips to Cairns—once to see a doctor, and once to see a dentist. I said, "When do I have to go?"

"End of this coming April, Jim. That'll give you plenty of time to get used to the idea."

"But I don't really want to go."

"Oh, it's no use talking like that. You should have been at a proper school long before now. Don't you want to have an education? Live in a city like a civilized man with a good profession at your fingertips?"

"No. I don't mind being educated, but I don't want to live in a city. I want to live here on Oonaderra."

"Well, you will one day, Jim, when the property

becomes yours. Who knows, I might even shift to the city later on with your mother and let you run the property. But in the meantime, you must go to school."

"Couldn't we get one of those private tutors they advertise in *The Cattleman*?"

"No, Jimmy. Can't you see? You've got to get away from this place before you finish up like those bloody boongs!"

"Well, I'd rather finish up like an Aborigine than like some of the white men I read about. And what about yourself, you're always telling Mum that the city people are nothing but a mob of rogues? What if I turn out to be like that?"

He walked down the lines of saddles and began running his hands over them, while thinking of a way of replying to my outburst. Then he came back to the table and perched himself on the same edge. He took off his Stetson, peered into it and said, "I know I've said that, and I really do believe some city people are like that, but you've still got to live with other people. Which brings me to another thing." He looked up.

"What, Dad?"

"Well . . . er . . . well, you know . . . you're growing up now . . . you've got to get used to mixing with white girls . . . your mother and I don't want to see you end up chasing those young gins for a pastime. You know what sex is all about, don't you?"

"Should I?" I mumbled in my confusion.

"Of course you should! That's what I'm trying to tell you about now."

"Well, why are you trying to tell me if I'm supposed to know all about it?"

"For god's sake! Don't make it any harder for me than it is already. What I mean is, you've seen the bulls running with the cows, and you've seen the camp dogs trying to get at Trudy when she's that way, haven't you?"

In my innocence, I had never associated animals

mating as being an embarrassing subject to speak of, as my father was demonstrating.

I told him I knew all about that sort of thing, but sex, to me, meant either male or female.

Dad stuck his hat back on his head in futile disgust, both at the matter he couldn't speak of and at my ignorance of the facts of life. He got off the table and said, "You won't say anything to your mother about our man-to-man talk, will you, Jim?"

"No, Dad."

"Oh, by the way."

"Yes?"

"I think I'll tell Mum to let you have a few more days away from those lessons. You're ahead with them, aren't you?"

"Yes."

"Well, that's settled."

"Thanks, Dad. That'll be beaut!" I picked up the duck in the bag.

"Come on then," he said. "If we're going to eat that duck, we'd better get it cleaned."

We called Trudy and closed the shed.

As we walked over the rise, I couldn't help thinking about the future. I looked at Dad walking ahead of me. How unlike we were. He was short and wiry, so much the grazier walking over his wide domain; and me, his red-haired son and already as tall as him. We had nothing in common, except our love of Oonaderra. This was our home, and he had ruled that I should leave it.

To this day, the smell, or just the thought, of wild duck fills me with a reasonless dread of the unknown.

THREE

NEXT MORNING, while my father went over to the saddle shed to harness Nellie to the big wooden slide for snigging the firewood to the house, I had to help Mum before the women came to the washhouse at the foot of the rise. The washhouse, open on all four sides, had a galvanized iron roof for shade and to catch rainwater, which ran off it into the iron tank alongside to supply water for the washing and rinsing in the tubs under the roof. It had always been my job to fill the copper by the tank and light the fire under it, and to help my mother carry the baskets of washing over from the house.

I had the fire going in no time at all, because I wanted to help Dad with the snigging and ride on top of the loads of wood.

The last basket of washing was ready on the kitchen floor, and Mum said, "Here's Alice and Minnie coming now. You bring their breakfast there on the table and that billy of tea on the stove; I'll take this basket."

"Righto, Mum."

I gathered up the billy and the two plates, each piled with a slab of cold corned beef and leftovers from our last night's dinner, and on top of each heaped plate was a thick slice of bread and plum jam. I followed Mum over to the washhouse.

" 'Lo, Missus; 'lo, Jimmy," the two women greeted us. They were sitting on the washhouse floor, smoking their pipes.

"Hello, Alice; hello, Minnie," Mum answered.

I, too, answered their greeting, but I called them by their proper tribal names: Alipjira and Tomini.

While Mum filled the boiler with the first of the washing, I gave the women their breakfast. I thought how incongruous, even ridiculous, the women looked in their bare feet and crumpled floral frocks they were wearing, two sizes too big for them. They were handouts from my mother. She, by contrast, looked beautiful in her white sandals, short-sleeved red gingham frock, and the wide-brimmed white straw hat she always wore when outdoors to protect her complexion.

"Come on, Jimmy, if you want to go with Dad, you had better get a move on. Run a cloth over the clotheslines for me and then you can go."

I got a cloth and ran it over the lines stretched between the two big mango trees at the back of the washhouse.

Just then, Dad came over the rise. He was standing on the platform of the slide which was fashioned out of a big tree fork with its end adzed to form an upturned front. A heavy iron ring was bolted to this for taking the coupling of the swingletree on Nellie's harness chains.

Dad stopped at the boiler to have a word with Mum. "Let the gins do all the hard yakka," he said. "They'll sit there in the damned shade all day and let you do all the work if you don't stir the lazy buggers up. Come on, you two!" he shouted at the women. "You want to stay there all day! You want 'bacca by and by. Me no give you suppose you no get washing finished quick."

"Yes, Boss." The two women stuffed the remainder of their food into their mouths and scrambled up to start work.

"Oh, don't worry, Jack," Mum said. "I can handle them."

"OK, then. Come on, Jimmy."

I hopped up onto the slide. The axes were on it ready for the cutting of the firewood to tide us over the coming Wet. We set off for the timber at the back of the camp.

There was always something exciting happening whenever we were getting firewood over in the heavy timber behind the camp. If it wasn't wild pigs being bailed up by the camp dogs, it would be 'roos or wallabies going for their lives out to the open forest country beyond the lagoon. Six-foot-long goannas that looked, at first sight, like crocodiles instead of the lizards they were, could often be seen scrabbling up the trees after birds' eggs, especially those of the bronzewing and Torres Strait pigeons. Once my father and I watched a huge goanna finishing off the remains of a dead calf left by the crows. It took the bones of the calf in its mouth and pushed them down its throat by ramming them against the log the remains were lying beside. And there were more than enough snakes in that place, too, because it was near water. And crocodiles (alligators we call them) lurked in the deep waterholes along the creek.

Dad pulled up and looked around for the men, who had not yet arrived to start work. We got off the slide. He never took kindly to being held up by Aborigines. He cupped his hands to his mouth and "coo-eed" in the direction of the camp. A few minutes later, the five men Tajalli had promised to send came walking through the trees, obviously as reluctant to begin swinging axes as my father was determined they would.

"You take plurry long time," he snapped at them. "If you no get a move on quick smart, me tell policeman send you longa Palm Island, may be Yarrabah. You lazy fella too much. Maybe me belt you longa stock-whip. Get a move on!" Threats of police and mission stations always worked.

They set to work with the axes on the tree limbs and logs lying around, cutting the wood into stove lengths. When sufficient wood had been cut, Dad ordered two of the men to load the slide. They piled the wood in a double layer about three feet high and then capped it with a "jockey" layer along the middle to take the chain for tying the load down.

Dad then walked ahead while I scrambled on top and took the reins. I flicked them along Nellie's back, "Giddup!" and away she went, hauling the load to the woodheap behind the washhouse.

The unloading of the slide was a simple matter. We let the horse pull it up along the foot of the rise behind the first mango tree, where the load was tilted enough for Dad to knock the pin out of the chain and let the wood tip itself off the slide. And away we would go for the next load.

After the third trip we returned just in time to witness what, for a white man, might have been a quick death. I saw one of the men pause in his chopping of a hollow log to split it with his axe. He sank the blade into the middle of it and reached over to lever the axe out for the next stroke. While he was bent over, a two-foot-long death adder crawled out of the log near his feet. I shouted, "Look out! Snake!" But the man's foot touched the adder which instantly swept its head and tail round his ankle and sunk in its fangs.

The man kicked it away, and one of the other men killed it with his axe. Then, as calmly as if he were tying a shoelace, he sat down and drew his ankle up to his mouth and sucked the venom from the fang holes and spat it out. Then he stood up and said, "That fella snake no more bite nobody. Him make good fella tucker; by and by, cook 'im longa fire."

The man who had killed the snake hung it on the limb of a sapling, and the work of cutting and loading went on.

Just before lunch, and the last load, another episode took place. The men had loaded the slide and were putting their axes on top of the wood. One of them yelled out, "Pundarra! Pundarra!" He had caught sight of a carpet snake, over twenty feet long, lying in a huge coil in the shade at the foot of a big ironbark. The man took a long, straight piece of timber, about twice the thickness of a walking stick, and sharpened one end. He went over toward the tree and then hurled the pointed stick with all his force. It took the snake between the eyes, right through its head. It uncoiled out from the foot of the tree in a convulsive flash and lay undulating and heaving its massive body.

Dad and I and the other men walked over to have a look at it. In the center of its body was a huge swelling caused by the meal it had swallowed within the last few hours. "What that fella eat?" Dad asked the man.

The man ran his hand over the swelling, grinned, and said, "Him eat big fella wallaby. You want skin belonga this fella snake, Boss?"

"All right. When you skin 'im let me have it. What you do longa snake meat?"

"Make it good fella tucker, Boss. Cook him snake, cook wallaby longa 'im belly."

"Well, all you fella come longa washhouse," Dad said. "Missus cook tucker; all you get tucker, 'bacca for make it good fella work longa firewood."

They put their axes on the load and followed us, but they came no closer to the house than the washhouse. While we unloaded the slide, they sat with the two women who had finished the washing and were waiting, like the men, for their meal and the gift of two extra sticks of tobacco each.

Dad took Nellie and the slide back over the rise to unharness her and let her go. I went over to the house to get the big billy of curried stew that my mother had made for the two women and the men. I took with it a loaf of bread, plates, spoons, and a billy of tea.

Now that the work was over, the Aborigines were sitting, relaxed and chattering, in a circle on the wash-house floor.

One of the men, Tipunta, said to me, "Alipjira and Tomini"—he pointed at the two women—"say they like keep you longa them, longa camp. They like you. No have pickaninny, now want you pickaninny belonga them." He roared with laughter. But I didn't mind being called a pickaninny (all uninitiated boys, and girls, are called that by their tribal elders, and I was still, to them, an uninitiated boy). I set the things down and said, keeping in with their mood of fun, "By and by, me all same Tajalli; make you get big fright longa me. You no more laugh then."

The whole seven of them roared with merriment at the joke, and I left them, eating and laughing, to go to the house for my own lunch. Afterward, Dad sent me over with the trade tobacco he had promised the men and the two sticks each for the women.

The Aborigines had washed up after their meal and had stacked the plates in one of the tubs ready to be taken back to the house. But I had not been told to bring them back straightaway, and in any case I was free for the rest of that day, so I followed the men and women. They went to skin the carpet snake and the death adder. I went on to the camp where Tajurra met me. It was about one o'clock.

We wandered around the camp, then stopped to talk with old Tirkalla and Ninji sitting by the fire outside their mia-mia.

We had not been there more than five minutes

when a silence suddenly fell over the whole camp. It was tense, electrical—like the silence following a lightning flash before the thunder.

Tajalli came racing up through the mia-mias, shouting, "Obija inkali Rimpunta! Obija inkali Rimpunta!" ("Smoke signals from the Rimpunta tribe!"). He stopped beside us, pointing through the trees away to the south. All eyes, including mine, swung to read the smoke signals rising far away up into the sky. I couldn't even see any smoke. But Tajurra could. He said, "Policeman come; got two fella tracker longa him."

From nowhere, Nimapadi and the six men, the ones I had seen helping at the initiation of the boys on the night of the corroboree, came crowding around us.

Tajalli spoke rapidly to them—too rapidly for me to understand what he was saying. But they immediately began calling to the rest of the tribe, urging them to hurry.

Like shadows, the six men left us and fled up into the timber behind the camp, followed by every man, woman, and pickaninny, carrying blankets and whatever else they could manage in their panic. It was fantastic the way they melted away and vanished through the trees in the direction of the lagoon. Even the camp dogs had gone.

Only Tajalli, Nimapadi, the old couple, Tajurra, and myself were left.

Tajalli squatted down to speak to the old man and Ninji. He spoke rapidly. The old man was nodding eagerly at what was being said, and old Ninji, too, was responding in the same fashion. The conversation lasted no more than two minutes. Then Tajalli rose to his feet and ran with Nimapadi towards the beach.

The old couple were smoking contentedly on a full pipe of tobacco.

Tajurra nudged me to follow him.

We went down through the camp and around behind Tajalli's mia-mia to watch him and Nimapadi making ready to leave in a canoe moored to the creek bank. It was a long dugout that had been fashioned from a big red-cedar log by burning and hollowing out its interior. Its anchor was a rock on the end of a long bark rope.

Tajalli and Nimapadi, carrying their long hunting spears, knives, and a paddle each, were just clambering aboard. I saw a bailer shell and an old gin bottle lying in the bottom of the dugout alongside a string dillybag.

The two men dropped their spears and knives down in the dugout. Tajalli undid the mooring rope from the prow. Then both took their paddles and began guiding the dugout along the creek to the open sea.

Tajurra and I followed down to the beach to watch them. "Where are they going?" I asked.

"Longa reef. Longa deep fella water."

"Why they take knife, take spear?"

"They make big fella dive longa deep fella water. Take spear and hit 'im shark longa nose; make him fright, make him go away."

"What they go for?"

"Barata."

"Barata? What this fella barata?"

"Barata live longa deep fella water." Tajurra made a long, slow downward motion of his hand to indicate a great. depth of water.

Then I remembered his previous mention of the use of barata as a tribal right of the leader to perform euthanasia—a quiet and easy death—upon any member of his tribe, if the circumstances warranted it. The approaching police party and the inevitable recapture of old Tirkalla, to take him back to the mission station, was now driving Tajalli to procure the barata. He would save his father from dying within the four walls of a mission-station cell block.

I looked at Tajurra standing beside me. His face

46

was impassive; his deep-set eyes were looking at the men in the dugout now approaching the outer reef.

I don't know how I really felt; there were so many conflicting emotions in me. But I do remember the strange sadness that came over me when I looked at Tajurra, my lifelong friend. It was an uneasy sadness for something I could not quite comprehend. I said to him, "How long before this fella policeman come longa Oonaderra?"

With absolute certainty, he answered, "Two hour maybe little bit more if he stop longa your house, talk longa your people."

"How long this barata stay longa man before him die?"

" 'Bout an hour, maybe bit more."

"It make man sick longa pain?"

"No more; man sleep."

"Tajurra?"

"Yes, Jimmy?"

"Suppose this fella policeman find out Tajalli give bad fella drink longa Tirkalla, Tajalli get in big fella trouble; policeman take him longa prison?"

"Policeman no know, Jimmy. By and by, when man die, barata no more stop longa him. Suppose man give barata longa pig; by and by, pig die; man eat pig; no more barata longa pig; him good fella tucker."

He meant that after death from barata poisoning the flesh of any animal, including man, would convert the properties of the poison into normal body fluids. It was, as proved later, an undetectable poison.

Tajurra did not seem inclined to talk, so we went and sat in the shade of the pandanus palms to watch the two men, who by that time had paddled the dugout through the only channel in the reef to the deep seaward side of it.

We watched them in the distance as they dropped the rock anchor. Then Tajurra said, "Tajalli dive now."

We saw the two men stand up, spears in their hands. Then Tajalli dived overboard and disappeared.

For about two minutes the dugout, with Nimapadi standing in the prow, spear at the ready, lifted and rose as the swells rolled under it to break on the white sand fringing the reef.

Suddenly Tajalli's head rose above the water, and Nimapadi reached out to take his spear and the loaded dillybag on the point of it. Then he pulled Tajalli out of the water into the dugout.

The men began working and intermittently throwing overboard whatever it was they had brought up from deep water.

They finished their task and came back with the wind behind them, their paddles dipping and flashing in the sunlight as the dugout scudded across the quieter water between the reef and the beach.

Tajurra whispered for me to sit still until the two men had run the dugout back to its mooring in the creek and gone back to the old man and Ninji.

Then we followed. Tajalli, now carrying his shield in one hand and the gin bottle in the other, and Nimapadi, carrying something in his hand, were hurrying up ahead of us.

When we had almost reached the two men, Tajurra stopped me. Tajalli and Nimapadi knelt down in front of the old couple still seated by their fire.

Tajurra put his finger to his lips for me to remain silent as we edged our way over to lean against a tree to watch what was about to take place.

Tajalli laid his shield across the old man's knees. The painting of Oona, the great turtle, lay uppermost.

The old man placed his thin hands on the shield, over the painted symbol of his tribe, and closed his eyes. Ninji sat beside him, impassive and waiting.

Next Tajalli spat into the palm of his hand and reached across to rub the saliva over the cicatrices on the old man's upper arms and chest.

Then I saw the things Nimapadi had been carrying. They lay on the ground beside him: a pair of beeli sticks and the gold-lip pearl shell I had seen him use for catching the boys' blood on the night of the corroboree. Inside the pearl shell lay a small, brilliant red-and-yellow-banded purra shell.

Tajalli scooped up a handful of white ash from the fire as Nimapadi picked up the beeli sticks, one in each hand, and began to beat them rhythmically one against the other, first the right stick against the left and vice versa, to alternate the distinct sound made by each.

While the rhythmic beating of the beeli sticks went on, Tajalli began to sprinkle the white ash over the old man's chest and arms, chanting softly, "Oona, Oona, Myee Oona. Oona, Oona, Oona, Myee Oona."

The white ash collected on the wetted cicatrices of old Tirkalla's tribal marks until the raised scars stood out stark-white against the black skin.

Next Tajalli took the looped cord from his hair and fastened it around the old man's snowy-white hair in the tribal manner of a reigning elder.

Nimapadi kept up his beating of the beeli sticks. All the while Ninji stared in front of her.

Tajalli stopped chanting and said, "Miaja Kadi! Myee Wundul!"

The old man opened his eyes and kept his hands pressed to the shield while Tajalli spoke rapidly to him in words unknown to me. The old man nodded and spoke the same words to Ninji, who nodded as vigorously as he had done.

Then Tajalli spoke to Nimapadi, who immediately stopped his beating of the beeli sticks. He put them down, and picked up the pearl shell with the purra shell in it and held them out for Tajalli, who took the purra shell.

Tajurra's restraining hand kept me from going forward in my impatience to see what I sensed was imminent—the offering of the barata.

49

In the ashes by the side of the fire was Ninji's battered old black billy, about one third filled with tea, which I think she had made specially for that occasion.

Tajalli lifted the gin bottle from the ground in front of him and held it up for the old man and Ninji to look at. I saw that it held about a quarter inch of pale pinkish, almost colorless fluid. There seemed hardly enough there, I thought, for it to do what it was supposed to. I didn't realize that its potency was far, far greater than the small proportion indicated.

The old man and Ninji both nodded again with the same eagerness I had seen previously. Tajalli lowered the bottle and pulled out the cork. With the bottle in one hand and the purra shell in the other, he carefully poured the barata into it until it was full to the brim. Then he tipped the barata from the shell into the billy of tea and stirred the mixture several times with his finger to thoroughly mix it.

Nimapadi then handed him the gold-lip pearl shell. He took it and poured approximately half of the warm mixture of tea and barata into it.

Impatiently the old man lifted his hands from the shield and took the pearl shell from Tajalli. He raised it to his lips and swallowed the drink in one quick gulp. He smiled and handed the pearl shell back to Tajalli who filled it with the remainder of the mixture from the billy.

Ninji, pathetic old Ninji, was reaching out for her share in the manner that Tirkalla had done before her. Her face was twitching like a child both expecting and fearing the loss of a gift anticipated for so long.

Tajalli, her son, did not keep her waiting long. He passed the pearl shell into her frail hands. For a moment, such was her eagerness for the drink I thought she would spill it, but, no, she raised the shell to her lips and drank. Then she smiled and gave it back to Tajalli.

When the ritual was over, I felt a curious sense of letdown. Tajalli and Nimapadi seemed to be as casual about the approaching death of the old people as it is possible to imagine. It seemed to me that the act of taking human life was no more to them than an everyday occurrence carried out without passion or pity, which, of course, according to their tribal customs, was precisely as it was meant to be. Necessity had governed them and shaped their laws since time immemorial. So they had performed, without outward emotion, their duty in accordance with those laws.

Although I felt uneasy and unsure about something I could not fully understand, I was not averse to aligning myself with Tajalli's people whose customs I had come to assimilate.

Ninji and Tirkalla calmly lit their pipes with a live coal from the fire and began to puff away contentedly. Tajalli was talking to them in a quiet voice while Nimapadi went across to the creek with the billy, the bottle, and the shells to wash them free of the barata.

He came back and put the empty billy on the ground near the fire. Tajalli took his shield off the old man's knees and walked away with it and Nimapadi down toward the beach. Both men knew that Tajurra and I had been there all the time, but neither had made any sign that our presence had been resented.

Tajurra walked out to the edge of the camp with me and said, "Tajalli no worry longa you now, Jimmy; him know you same as brother belonga me; all the same Oona man. Him know you no tell nobody 'bout barata."

"No, I no tell nobody," I said and looked curiously back at the old couple—they were smoking and talking and evidently quite happy.

"What you do, Tajurra," I asked, "when policeman come longa here, ask you 'bout old man, old woman?"

"Policeman no talk longa me, Jimmy. Him talk longa Tajalli, longa Nimapadi."

"What you do longa old people when they die?"

He answered, "Leave 'im longa ground all night. By and by spirit inside old people get out; him run, look longa Dreamtime longa Oona—big fella turtle live longa sky. Him stop, no more come back."

The Dreamtime, the Aborigines' heaven, seemed little different from the heaven of which my mother talked and which she herself firmly believed in. I accepted both as being the same, except that Tajurra didn't have to say prayers every night and I did.

Then Tajurra mentioned casually that he and his people would shortly be going on their Walkabout. They did this every year, just as they had always done. Two, maybe three days before the Wet set in, they would leave the camp for the great circuit of their wanderings in search of the lily bulbs and the lush feeding to be found in the great lagoons and waterways, with their myriads of birds and all the variety of natural seasonal foods Aborigines crave and seek.

"When you go?" I asked.

"Maybe three, maybe four day before big fella rain come."

"How you know when rain come Tajurra?"

"No know. Tajalli make big fella rain come when all Oona people go Walkabout."

And it was true, the tribe always left two or three days ahead of the cyclones that sweep in from over the Coral Sea, bringing the flood rains that can last up to three months or more before they end. After the Wet, the tribe would return to their camp site to rebuild their mia-mias after my father had burned them down. No Aboriginal would ever use his mia-mia again after his tribe had returned from Walkabout—"too many big fella debbil-debbils hide longa camp" was Tajurra's explanation.

Then he said, "Better you go longa house, longa your people, Jimmy. Policeman soon come; better 'im no see you friend belonga me."

I saw there was sense in that, so we promised to

meet later and I went home. But the events of that day were far from over. And I was determined to be at the camp when the police party got there.

FOUR

IT IS incredible that my parents were not aware of what was happening on Oonaderra at that time. They had not the faintest idea of what I knew and had seen. But they were too remote from the Oona people to know or really care what happened to them. As long as the Aborigines were available to do the work required of them in the running of the property, that was all that mattered to my parents. To have suggested to my father that the Aborigines had evolved a culture rich in human values, so manifestly embodied in their tribal laws for those who would take the trouble to understand them, would have enraged him into a furious denunciation of them. I think my father would have been shocked had he known that the man whom my grandparents had orphaned fifty years before had returned to Oonaderra like a hunted animal, when all he wanted was to die on the land of his forefathers and be buried in the sacred grove of his people.

And the Curse that old Tirkalla himself had initiated so long ago had reached out, or so it would seem, over half a century to draw him back within the orbit of its power.

Even then, the pursuing police party were traveling from the south, relentlessly tracking down their quarry—an old man who would never again run from danger. . . .

I had helped my mother to bring the dry washing back to the house. We were all sitting on the back veranda in the big wicker armchairs. My father was smoking and reading; he had his feet up on the veranda rail.

Mum and I were seated by the table, looking out at the willie wagtails swooping down from the orange tree to torment Trudy, who was lying in the shade of the lemon tree opposite. Mum said, "Just look at that."

The wagtails had turned from worrying the dog to dart at Suney, our Siamese cat, stalking a pair of peewees that were strutting around the lawn looking for grass grubs. All the cat got for her pains was a swift, short flight of the birds "peeweeing" their anger, and then they swooped back and down to give her a couple of stabs on the rump. She let out the most ungodly caterwauling and started the dog barking and every magpie, crow, currawong, and kookaburra in the vicinity joined its call to the general alarm.

"What the blazes has that damned cat been up to now?" Dad snapped angrily, looking up from his book.

"You know Suney, Jack," Mum answered, and Dad went on with his reading as quietness again settled over the place.

How serene everything looked. The flower beds at both sides of the lawn were massed with daisies, gerberas, marigolds, and Mum's pride—her roses. The big Dorothy Perkins that climbed over the arched entrance to the veranda was in full bloom, the perfume from its clusters of pink blooms blending in with the smell of honeysuckle that grew along the south side of the veranda. I was watching a colony of the little native black bees flitting over the roses; their soft buzzing, the perfume, and the quiet warmth of the afternoon were almost sending me to sleep.

The grandfather clock in the corner of the front room behind us began to strike the hour. I listened, eyes closed, to the whir and sound of the gong striking three o'clock.

Suddenly Trudy barked a warning of someone approaching. She barked again, "pointing" across to the rise. We all followed her gaze.

Coming over the rise was the police party: a mounted police trooper, two mounted Aboriginal trackers, leading a packhorse loaded with their bedding and rations, and behind the packhorse was tethered a spare mount, saddled and bridled.

The party stopped at the washhouse where the two trackers dismounted. They tied the horses to the posts of the washhouse and sat down in its shade. The trooper came riding over to us.

I had seen him about a year before when he called at Oonaderra with census papers to take particulars about the property. He was wearing the police trooper's uniform: brown boots, khaki pants and shirt, and the familiar "Digger's" hat with the side brim turned up and clipped in place by his Queensland Police badge.

"Good day, there!" he called out.

Mum and Dad answered, "Good day, Pat." I answered with just a "Good day." I knew what he had come for and I didn't like him because of it.

"What brings you all the way out here, Pat?" Dad asked.

Before the trooper could answer, Mum said, "How about coming in out of the sun and having a cup of tea, Pat, before you start on whatever it is you're here for?"

"Thanks, Missus. That's very good of you."

He dismounted, dropped the reins to trail on the ground to keep the horse from straying, and came up onto the veranda. I got up and gave him my chair and sat on the rail.

He was a huge man with a freckly face. He took off his hat and dropped it on the floor beside him. Like me, he had ginger hair.

"Something special you're here for, Pat?" Dad asked again.

"No, not really, Jack; we're after a damned Abo. He got away from Palm Island, and we've had one helluva time picking up his tracks. It took those boys of mine"—he was referring to the Aboriginal trackers—"all of two blasted days to locate his tracks before we could get started. I know what I'd like to do to him when I catch him."

"What's his name?" Dad enquired.

"Willie Winkle."

I almost cried out in protest at the degrading name they had given poor old Tirkalla.

"Never heard of him," Dad said.

"He's here all right, Jack. We followed his tracks right through past the lagoon. He'll be holed up somewhere in the camp. But I'll soon get him when I go over there."

I looked away in disgust from the big hulking man. For a moment a crazy idea took hold of me: his horse was standing side-on to me near the veranda rail. In the saddle holster his rifle butt poked up invitingly. I could have had that rifle and shot him in less than two seconds; it was silly of me, but my mother came out with tea and cake and saved him, and me, from an imaginary end.

Over tea, the policeman said, "Your boongs been giving you any trouble lately, Jack?"

My father was quick to avoid any statement that might endanger or threaten to deplete his labor force.

"No, Pat. My mob are as quiet as lambs—never a bit of trouble with them at all."

"Well, that's just as I hoped it would be, Jack. But you know as well as I do what those boongs are like once you start to be decent to them. They're as likely as not to sink a tomahawk into your skull the moment you turn your back to them. Give the swine nothing, I say. Put the fear of Christ into them and never let up on them."

"I think you're right there, Pat."

"You bet I am!"

Evidently the policeman had an obsessional grudge against all Aborigines. Or maybe he was being as careful as my father was to side with vested interests and authority. Graziers also have more money, as a rule, than the Aborigines.

After they had talked for a little while, I managed to slip away into the kitchen without my mother or the men realizing I had gone. I wanted to get over to the camp to warn Tajalli that the police party had arrived. Tajalli and the others, however, were well aware of it long before I was.

I cut three pieces off the cake in the kitchen and wrapped them in paper. Circling round the front of the house, I made my way up the side of the flower beds and over to the washhouse without being called back.

The two trackers, who were, of course, detribalized, were both dressed exactly the same as the policeman. They were sitting smoking and talking. I just wanted to have a look at them.

"Good day," I said. "How you do?"

"G'day," they answered. "Pretty good."

I was not inclined to yarn with them, so I went on over to the camp, near Tajalli's mia-mia in search of him or Tajurra. No one was there. Then I saw Tajalli and Nimapadi standing up near the old couple's mia-mia. Both men were wearing their drover's boots, khaki pants, and shirts—the outfits supplied by my father to the men to wear when riding and mustering the cattle during most of the year.

I went through the camp to them. They turned their heads at my approach; but instead of their usual greeting, they remained straight-faced and silent. They turned away from me to look at the old people who were lying on a blanket, covered by another one pulled up to their chins.

I looked at the old man and Ninji. Their faces seemed not to have changed. Their eyes were open, although I don't think they were really looking at anything. They were smiling with such ineffably gentle smiles that I thought they were not going to die. But within a minute or two, first the old man's and then Ninji's mouth opened and slowly, as though they were falling asleep, they both whispered, "Oona, Oona, Myee Oona . . ." Their mouths closed, and for a moment or so their eyelids flickered and then closed.

I was standing beside Tajalli. He said softly, "Myee Oona" and stepped back to allow Nimapadi to draw the blanket up over the faces.

For the first time in my life I had seen human death. All my previous notions about its horror, its imagined ugliness were completely banished now that I witnessed its quiet visitation on two people who looked, in death, more at peace than they would ever have been in life. It was a moment of revelation and relief which has left its impression on me to this day.

Nimapadi spoke to Tajalli who turned to me. "More better you hide, Jimmy. Policeman come now."

I looked over through the trees and saw the trooper on his horse cantering across toward us. The trackers were not with him. Tajalli pointed to the tree that Tajurra and I had leaned against before. "You stay longa tree," he said.

By circling around it, I was able to keep hidden when the trooper rode up to the two men and reined in his horse, which was snorting and backing away from the smell of death. The trooper managed to calm it; then he said, "Where is boss fella longa this place?"

"Me, Boss," Tajalli answered.

"Fella belonga Palm Island stop longa you?"

"Yes, Boss."

"Where him hide?"

"Him no more hide, Boss. Him dead. An' woman belonga him dead."

"You lying swine! Where is he? Where is the woman?"

Tajalli walked over and drew the blanket away from the old people's faces.

The trooper stared down in disbelief; then he got down to inspect them.

He opened their mouths and carefully looked inside them. He opened their eyes and carefully scrutinized them, too. He drew the blanket off them and checked them all over before he was satisfied and straightened up.

"Cover 'em up!" he snapped.

Nimapadi covered the old people with the blanket again.

The trooper took out his notebook and pencil. "What your fella name?" he asked Nimapadi.

"Boss call me Paddy, Boss."

"What yours?" he asked Tajalli.

"Boss call me Charley, Boss."

He scribbled the names down with what must have been details and remarks about the finding of the dead people, because there was a whole page full of writing. Then he put his notebook and pencil back into his shirt pocket and remounted. From his vantage point he said to Tajalli, "When you bury 'em?" He jerked his head down at the blanket over the old people.

"Longa morning, Boss."

"Well, see that you damn well do, or I'll be out again to take the bloody lot of you back to Palm Island.

Get those bastards buried before they stink the place out! And where are other people belonga this place?" he snapped. Tajalli told him they were out gathering food. "All right," he said and rode away back to the house.

I came from behind the tree and gave Tajalli and Nimapadi a piece each of the cake I had been holding. They thanked me and ate it while they watched the trooper dismounting at the house.

Then Tajurra appeared from nowhere. I gave him the other piece of cake.

When Tajalli saw the trooper walk on to the veranda, he cupped his hands to his mouth, and I was astonished at the way he mimicked the call of a swamp pheasant: "Woop, woop, woop, woop, w-o-o-o-o-o-o-o-o-o-p!"

Instantly the pheasants that feed and nest near the lagoon answered his call. He waited for them to stop. Then, clear and distinct in the distance, came the penetrating double-note of a mopoke owl repeated twice, "More-pork, more-pork." It was the answering call from Tajalli's people waiting for the "all clear" where they were in hiding up near the lagoon.

There was still another task to be done before the Oona people returned to the camp. Tajalli spoke to Tajurra and Nimapadi and said to me, "You want help Tajurra, Jimmy?"

"Yes."

"You bring spears longa mia-mia longa here."

Tajurra and I went around collecting the long hunting spears that were lying on the ground near the mia-mias, where they had been left when the men, women, and children had fled after the smoke signals had appeared in the sky, telling of the approaching police party.

We gathered a couple of dozen of the spears and brought them to Tajalli and Nimapadi, who drove them, points down, into the ground until they had surrounded the dead couple and their mia-mia in a fenced ring.

"What for they do this fella thing, Tajurra?" I asked.

He said, "Him stop spirit longa old people get out. Longa morning, take spear down, let spirit longa old people get out; this fella spirit run too fast altogether back longa sky, longa Oona, longa Dreamtime. By and by, longa morning, all women cry longa dead people; take 'im longa another place, put him longa big fella stones. All the time all the women make big fella cry. Put it fat, put it ash longa head. Too much cry altogether."

Tajurra's description of holding the spirits of the dead couple within the circle of upraised spears was understandable enough to me, but I could not fathom why the women would be putting fat and ashes on their heads. The wailing of the women when there was a death in the camp was something I had heard on more than one occasion, and I knew what it meant because my father would always have to write a report for the Department of Native Affairs explaining who had died and from what cause. I had read those reports two or three times before the mailman came and picked them up with our mail. They were always the same: Race: Aboriginal; Sex: Male or female; Cause of death: Influenza, dysentery, diarrhea, and once diphtheria; accidental death accounted for some of the Oonas.

I cannot recall a death from old age and most of the deaths were of children. I had never been present at a burial. Once I had been out shooting bronzewings with a .22 with Tajurra up past the lagoon. I had shot one in a tall stringybark and run to get it where it had fallen at the foot of the tree.

Tajurra yelled for me to come back. I never did get that dead pigeon, and Tajurra made it clear, but not why, that that place was taboo to us. But it was, as

I later found out, taboo to all children. Tajurra, at that time, had not been initiated into manhood, and for him to enter or even mention the place would have meant severe punishment. I found out for myself why the place was taboo.

Tajalli and Nimapadi went over to the creek bank and brought back the two halves of a mussel shell. They tied the shells to two spear shafts facing across the circle, in line with the heads of the old couple, and left the shells dangling on the long woven human-hair string to which they had tied them; then both men walked toward the beach.

"What that shell for, Tajurra?" I asked.

He said, "Two little fella boat for spirit belonga old people sail longa sky."

The sounds of the people returning to the camp could now be heard in direct contrast to the way they had departed and silently melted from sight in their headlong flight into the bush.

They came chattering and laughing, a little band of good-humored men, women, and children—till one woman spotted the upright ring of spears and the dangling mussel shells. She screamed, the short, frightening scream of an Aboriginal woman stricken with fear at being too close to a taboo ring and the sacred dead within it.

She turned and ran back to the group, away from the spirits which she knew still inhabited the bodies of old Tirkalla and Ninji.

In a dreadful sobbing and wailing, she sat herself on the ground, rocking back and forth in a slow pendulum movement. Her wailing went on and on, and then the other women, who had stopped in their tracks when they heard her scream, took it up until the camp was filled with their terrible lamentation for the dead.

It terrified me; like a waking nightmare, the sobbing of their grief rose and fell in a moaning upward and downward cadence, like a mourning wind of doom. I had heard it several times in the past, but from the house, never close like this.

Two of the sandy-haired mongrel camp dogs approached cautiously, their teeth bared in snarling uncertainty at having smelled the unfamiliar scent of human death.

The wailing was too much for me just to stand there listening to it. I said to Tajurra, "We go talk longa Tajalli, eh?"

He nodded and said, "By and by. Me want tell you 'bout Nimapadi."

He went on to explain that Nimapadi was Tajalli's twin brother, the last born of the two. Before the white people came to Oonaderra, he said tribal lore would have decreed the second-born child must die within the hour of its birth. This was done, he said, because it is the tribal belief that such children must go back to the Dreamtime to wait there until it is the right time to return to their mothers in the tribe; Nimapadi had survived only because the Aborigines had feared police action against them had they followed their tribal lore and been found out.

I later checked my grandfather's diaries in which he wrote about survey parties and police patrols operating in this area of the Peninsula when he first arrived to inspect the property before finally settling on it.

Tajurra finished telling me the story and said, "You no tell nobody I tell you about Nimapadi, all right?"

"All right," And we went on down to the beach and found the two men sitting under the pandanus palms, smoking their pipes.

Tajurra asked Tajalli if we could sit with him and Nimapadi.

"What for you want sit down longa here?" Tajalli asked.

"Jimmy want talk longa you."

Tajalli motioned with his hand for us to sit down facing him and Nimapadi, and said, "What for you want talk longa me, Jimmy?"

As Tajurra and I sat ourselves down cross-legged on the sand, I answered, "Tajurra tell me Oona people soon go Walkabout. When you go, Tajalli?"

He thought for a moment or two and looked out at the sky over the Coral Sea. Then he looked at me and said, "Maybe by and by, two, three fella day me tell big fella rain come longa this place; by and by, maybe four, five day, big fella rain come longa Oonaderra."

"How you make rain come longa this place?" I asked.

"Me sing longa teji stone, longa shiny stone, longa turtle; by and by, Oona, big fella turtle longa sky, send rain longa big fella wind. Oona people go Walkabout find plenty water, plenty lily root, plenty good fella tucker longa bird, longa big water all about everywhere."

Tajurra, of course, had told me previously about the tribe's Walkabout. But now that the time for them to leave was drawing near, I began to feel really depressed. The effects of seeing human death for the first time, the callous attitude of the trooper, and finally the dreadful wailing that was still going on in the camp had brought my unhappy feelings painfully into focus, because the Oonas would soon be leaving on their annual Walkabout of perhaps three months or more, leaving me without Tajurra and the others who were my mainstay against the loneliness of the bush. To make things worse, I, too, would be leaving to go to school in Brisbane. There would be so little time left, if any, after the Walkabout ended and the tribe returned to Oonaderra.

I said to Tajalli, "Suppose rain no more come this fella time, you no more go Walkabout?"

He laughed, "Rain come all right, Jimmy, me make it come maybe four, five day. Him come altogether plenty by and by."

Nimapadi grinned at me and asked, "What for you worry longa rain, longa Walkabout? You no want 'im Tajurra leave?"

I was quick to confirm what he said; I also told them about my having to go away to school.

They all began to speak at once.

"You no stop longa school all the time?" Nimapadi asked in dismay.

I nodded, and Tajalli said, "What for your father send you longa school, Jimmy? You no more want go longa school. You big fella now; you know all 'bout reading, writing. You know all thing 'bout ride horse, about chase 'im bullock, about put 'im brand longa cattle. You know plenty now."

I explained that my having to go to school was something I had no say in. I said it was the same as a Walkabout, only longer; and that I had to conform to my people's ways just the same as the Oona children had to conform to the tribal ways and to learn according to those ways. I pointed at Tajurra's slowly healing cicatrices as an example of how we must all learn how to grow up.

The two men nodded gravely, in total agreement that tribal customs, whether black man's or white man's, were there to be followed whether we like them or not.

Then the most surprising thing happened! I looked at Tajurra in disbelief; he was crying, quietly, without fuss, but the tears were running down his face. When I looked at him, he immediately brushed his hand across his eyes in a shamefaced gesture of trying to appear the man he was expected to be.

Before I could say anything, Tajalli said gently, "No more cry, Tajurra. Jimmy no forget you. Him come back by and by; him stay friend longa you all the time; him no forget."

66

Tajurra stood up and so did I. He pointed up to where we had been getting firewood that morning and said, "Men go get pundarra. You want come, see skin?"

I scrambled up, said something or other to the two men; then Tajurra and I went to see the men skinning the carpet snake.

It was the perfect chance for Tajurra to escape from the presence of his father and Nimapadi.

Although we never mentioned the incident again, the tears I had seen strengthened even more the bonds of our friendship.

The wailing of the women was dying away although the profound grief of all the Oonas continued. Eventually it ebbed out until only one woman kept the lament going softly, for the work of the living had still to be attended to.

Tajurra and I watched the men trying to skin the carpet snake—a job that had been delayed when the police party had made them take to the bush.

The men were fighting off two colonies of ants that had taken possession of the snake's body; pouring out of a nest near the tail was a column of savage bull ants; near its head another column of ferocious, big jumper ants were at work. Either way, the men were being savagely attacked as they dragged the body from the marauding ants' nests.

Skinning the snake was simple: one man heaved its head up and through the fork of a tree; another man then drove a makeshift spear through it to "lock" it into the fork.

While the other men straightened the body out, the first man slit around the back of the snake's head and ran the knife along the full length of its underside.

Then two of the men took hold of the skin behind the neck and walked backward, pulling it off as they went right to the end.

The man with the knife slit the belly and took out the full-grown wallaby. A shout from the man brought the women over with their coolamons to carry away the wallaby and the death adder.

The skin was stretched out over the ground and weighted with stones, while two of the men fetched salty mud and mangrove bark to shred and plaster over it with a final layer of wood ash to tan and preserve it during the twenty-four hours that was needed for the process and the handing over of the preserved skin to my father.

I left Tajurra and went home. The trooper had been invited to stay overnight, and he and the trackers had unsaddled their horses and hobbled them out to graze. The trackers had lit a fire to cook their meal outside the washhouse, where they would be sleeping.

Because the policeman no longer threatened the people on Oonaderra, I could relax and be less antagonistic toward him.

We had dinner by candlelight; afterwards the grown-ups settled down to enjoy one another's company and my father's best brandy, followed by port. I was offered only ginger beer.

They talked about the deaths at the camp. My father asked the policeman if he was sure the dead man was really the one he had been after. "Oh, yes, it's him all right. He has the scar around his neck to prove it. There was no mistaking that scar. Nothing suspicious about the deaths either, Jack, just a plain case of old age; although you can never be quite sure that those two old Abos haven't been pointed—you know how these Abos just lie down and die if they think somebody's 'pointed the bone' and 'sung' at them?"

Dad nodded and filled up the policeman's glass. I went to bed.

FIVE

THE TROOPER left immediately after breakfast in the morning. As he was leaving, he remarked to Dad, "Looks like the Wet's going to be late this year, Jack,"

"You think so?"

"Yair, look at that sky—not a sign of a cloud in it. We should have had a cyclone by now, the end of February."

"Well, I hope we're not going to miss out, Pat. The house tank's pretty low on water right now, and it won't take long for the creek and the lagoon to run dry in this heat."

"Yair, you need the rain all right. Well, hooray, Missus; hooray, Jack; and you look after yourself, Jimmy." He wheeled his horse and cantered over to the trackers who were mounted and waiting for him. At the top of the rise he waved to us and then led his party over it and out of sight.

Dad said to me, "What are you planning on doing today?"

"If it's all right with you," I answered, "I would like to ride over to the lagoon and see if I can pot a couple of pigeons for Mum to make one of her pies. OK, Dad?"

"Oh, I suppose so. But don't go shooting at every damn thing you see. And be careful you don't go scaring the daylights out of the cattle over there. And mind what you're doing with that rifle; leave the sights on it as they are. Use the long high-velocity bullets and you'll be sure to kill the birds with one shot. I don't want you firing at anything at too long a range and then leaving the damn thing wounded and dying out in the bush somewhere."

"OK, I'll be careful."

It was a strange thing about my father: he could be absolutely indifferent about the Aborigines over in the camp, but he would get distressed if an animal was suffering from a wound or lying helpless out in the bush for the crows to attack. He would abandon all thought for himself until he had found the unfortunate thing and put it out of its misery. It was quite beyond me to understand why he was like that. Mum, of course, was gentle and considerate about everything. With this gentleness she made our home on Oonaderra a place of love and comfort for Dad and me.

And I was never hesitant about imposing on her good nature. She said, "Come along, Jimmy." I followed her into the kitchen where she opened the big lolly tin and gave me a handful of boiled peppermints in a paper bag to take with me. "Now don't forget what your father has told you." Then she put her arms round me in a way that made me feel good inside.

Tajurra would not have thought much of me, if he had known my mother still kissed me. But he, too, often used to be kissed and fondled by Noola, his mother; I had seen her do it plenty of times before he was initiated. And all the other kids at the camp got plenty of loving and hugging from both their mothers and fathers.

I left Mum and wandered into what was once my grandfather's study where all the records of Oonaderra are kept as well as the gun cabinet with all the rifles and ammunition in it. I took my .22 repeater and a box of long cartridges on to the side veranda outside my bedroom window to clean the rifle and load the magazine.

Just as I was finishing the job I heard a curlew calling. I looked up. It was Tajurra. He was standing over in the trees by the side of the camp. He repeated the curlew call. I waved to let him know I wouldn't be long. Whenever he or I wanted to let each other know that something urgent was afoot, we would give the curlew call for either of us to hurry to where the other was.

I stuffed the box of cartridges and the bag of sweets into my shirt pocket, picked up the rifle, and slung it over my shoulder by its strap. I took a slice of bread from the kitchen and raced over the rise to the home paddock to saddle up my pony. Then I galloped over to the camp where Tajurra was waiting for me.

I dropped the reins over the pony's head and hopped down.

"What for you call me, Tajurra?" I asked.

"Tajalli say tell you come longa dead place, see grandfather, grandmother belonga me get put long big fella hole longa ground. You want come?"

"Me no more man," I said. "You tell me no let 'im boy see longa hole belonga dead people."

"Tajalli tell me all right now," Tajurra said. "Him say you all the same brother belonga me. You want to be man all the same me, come longa place belonga dead people?"

"All right," I said, "how you make me man?"

He opened his clenched hand and showed me a

human-hair cord the same as the one used to signify rank and manhood, and the same as the looped cord Tajurra himself was wearing around his hair. He put the cord across my forehead because my ginger hair was too short for tying. He looped and knotted it at the back of my head. And by that simple ceremony I was made man enough to be present at the sacred burial ground of the Oona tribe.

We left the pony with the reins trailing and went to Ninji's mia-mia. The circle of spears had been removed. The bodies had been wrapped in blankets and strapped with vines to two long poles: one body to each pole; these in turn were lashed to two transverse poles, one at either end, for carrying the bodies. Two cylindrical sheets of split tea-tree bark stood between the two wrapped bodies on the ground.

Tajalli and Nimapadi, both in their lap-laps, were squatting with spears in their hands at the feet of Tirkalla and Ninji. Tajalli's shield was on the ground beside him. He called out something, and six men, the ones I had seen at the corroboree, came from the vicinity of the unmarried men's long mia-mia, followed by eight women all wearing lap-laps. The women had their hair plastered down with goanna fat and wood ashes. The men were carrying spears.

They came to the side of the bodies. The women took their places at the ends of the transverse poles: four at the front and four at the rear. Two of the men picked up the bark cylinders. At a command from Tajalli, the women bent and lifted the bodies on the poles. The men lined up in single file and began to walk ahead. Tajalli, spear in one hand, shield in the other, went to the lead with Nimapadi behind and then the other men following.

Tajurra said, "We go now." We went over to the pony. Tajurra leapt up behind me in the saddle, and he was just in time or the pony would have bolted, because the women had begun their dreadful wailing again. The pony reared in fright and almost threw us, but we managed to hang on till it quietened down and set off, circling away from the line of men and women on their way to the burial place.

The burial place is no more than a mile and a half from the camp, but we were reluctant to reach it before the others and kept Creamy at a slow trot.

On catching sight of us, a flock of sulphur-crested white cockatoos rose from their feeding on the seed heads of the grass in a screeching, deafening yellow-and-white cloud of pounding wings. They steadily gained height and swung away to the north in a raucous, protesting flight.

The cattle, some of our white-faced Herefords, were grazing, spread out over the open forest country. Apart from lifting their heads as we passed, they paid no more attention to us. Farther on, a flight of squawking black cockatoos passed over us.

As we were rounding Cannon Ball Rock, the pony reared and stopped. Suddenly a mob of kangaroos went bounding past, directly in front of us. In the lead was an old man 'roo, moving in great bounds of thirty feet or more. The mob was there one moment, and the next it had vanished into the long grass among the trees.

We turned northwest from the Rock for the burial place about half a mile ahead of us. A hundred or so yards before we reached it, Tajurra said, "Better we leave horse longa here, Jimmy."

We dismounted and hitched the pony's reins to a sapling in the shade of a clump of blue gums and then walked the remainder of the way to the rocky gorge that leads down into the Oonas' burial ground.

Tajurra stopped me at the narrow cleft to the gorge's entrance and said, "Better stop longa here; take boot off."

We sat down, and I pulled my elastic-sided riding boots off and put them and the rifle to one side.

I had, of course, been to the burial ground before but never down the steep incline to the bottom of the gorge. The rocky sides are dotted with golden wattle trees and ghost gums which, in the early morning sunlight, throw their shadows in deep, long avenues of light and shade. Everything was so still and quiet. Not even a crow was there to break the silence of that gorge of the dead. I asked Tajurra if he had been down there.

"No bin down there. Too many debbil-debbil catch 'im boy, catch 'im girl down longa that fella place."

"Where they put 'im dead people?" I asked.

"Longa hole—that fella hole go down long ground all the same everywhere."

He was explaining that the foot of the gorge was lined on both sides with caves running back for long distances into the rock formation. Millions of years ago they had apparently been eroded out by the sea, which at one time must have covered Oonaderra.

Then we saw the burial procession slowly moving, with the women still wailing for the dead.

Tajurra and I stepped aside from the cleft as Tajalli came leading the way with his shield and his spear held before him. We waited for the procession to pass through the cleft, and then we fell in behind it for the steep descent down to the rock floor in the middle of the gorge. There the women lowered their burdens onto the flat rock surface and squatted in a line facing the bodies. Their wailing went on and on.

Tajurra and I sat some distance away behind the women. The men were standing to one side. The two with the bark cylinders stepped forward and placed them by the bodies. Tajalli spoke to Nimapadi, who undid the vine lashings holding the bodies to the poles. He drew the blankets aside to reveal old Tirkalla and Ninji. They looked so peaceful, so serene, it was hard to believe they were really dead.

The poles were taken away. Then two of the women went to the old man and two of them to Ninji. The wailing went on and on.

The women lifted the bodies into a sitting position. While one woman held the body of the old man upright from behind, the other bent up the knees under the chin. The other two women were doing the same to the body of Ninji. When the bodies had been drawn up into this bent-knees position, the other four women stood up to help hold the corpses while two of them picked up the split cylinders of bark.

Carefully, so as not to allow the bodies to lose their chin-over-knees position, the two women slipped the bark cylinders over the dead couple's heads and began to slide them gently down over the shoulders and arms while the other women gradually eased their hands downward to hold the position of the bodies until the cylinders had covered them completely.

Two of the men then bound the cylinders securely with the vines that had been used to lash the bodies to the poles. The women, still wailing in the same distraught way, stepped back to their places. The two men were holding the cylinders upright on the ground.

Tajalli stepped forward and touched the top of each cylinder, first with the point of his spear and then with the tip of his shield with the painting of Oona the great turtle facing downward.

The wailing of the women rose to a chant, and they began repeating over and over again, "Ninji, Ninji; Tirkalla, Tirkalla; Oona, Oona, Myee Oona." Their voices lifted higher and higher as two of the men walked over to a flat slab of rock resting against the foot of the almost perpendicular side of the gorge, opposite to where Tajurra and I were sitting. The flat rock, about three feet high and the same wide, was moved to one side to reveal a hole big enough for a man to crawl through. The two men picked up the cylinders and carried them to the entrance of the cave —one of the burial chambers.

I nudged Tajurra, who was at first reluctant to follow me, until my curiosity drove me closer to the entrance; then he came and stood behind me.

The entrance faces directly east, and the morning

sun was striking through the trees and sending a shaft of sunlight down into the recess of the cavern.

Tajalli and then Nimapadi crouched their way through the low entrance; and then, one by one, the other men passed through, and the last two handed the cylinders to the others inside then went in themselves.

Tajurra and I followed them inside, although by that time I was as scared as he was. The odor in the still atmosphere of the cavern was like that of old, very old musty books that have been locked away for years.

When my eyes had grown accustomed to the dim light from the sunlight suffused along the walls of the cavern, I saw the men, some distance away, lifting the cylinders onto a low ledge running along the foot of both walls. Outside the sound of the chanting women was faint and seemed far away.

Now I could see farther into the long recess of the burial chamber. There were scores of the tea-tree cylinders along both ledges, standing upright against the rock walls.

The men had placed the two cylinders in position and were coming back along the cavern. Tajurra and I hurried out through the narrow opening ahead of them.

Although we had been in there only a couple of minutes, the emergence into daylight was, for me, like coming into wakefulness from some dream beyond the bounds of reality.

The men came out, and the flat rock was pushed back into its place. The burial was over.

The women had stopped chanting and were crying softly while they gathered up the poles and the two blankets.

Tajalli and Nimapadi led the way out of the gorge. But Tajurra and I were well ahead of them. Neither he nor I wanted to be the last to get back up out of that gorge.

Outside the cleft entrance, I slipped on my boots

and slung the rifle over my shoulder. We went over to the pony and sat there on the ground for some time talking till I remembered the boiled sweets.

While Tajurra was eating, I was looking around for pigeons. Suddenly he stopped chewing and pointed. Less than a hundred yards away on the left, we could see a cow attacking and bellowing at something that was rushing at her.

Tajurra whispered, "Dingo. Two fella dingo try get calf belonga cow."

We mounted the pony without making any noise. Then we rode round in a wide arc till we reached a clump of trees no more than twenty paces from the dingoes. The wild dogs, big tawny-yellow brutes, looked up, but we were upwind from them, and they, being too intent on the calf, no doubt took the pony among the trees to be just a horse resting in the shade.

The cunning animals finally separated the calf from its mother, and one began to chase it in a wide circle away from her as the other kept attacking her to hold her there. The first dingo continued chasing the calf until it was exhausted and easier to kill. The cow was frantic.

I unslung the .22 and waited. The dingo left the cow and caught up with the other one. The calf swung round to come back to the cow. The dingoes followed, and one came directly into my sights. I fired. It dropped dead in its tracks and rolled over.

The other panicked, stopped, and looked around to locate the unseen danger. I lifted the sights on to it and fired. It staggered, recovered, and raced off in the direction of the creek.

"Hang on, Tajurra!" I shouted, and we set out after the wounded dingo at a full gallop. We were gaining on it when it reached the Big Waterhole. Blood was running from a wound in its withers where the bullet had hit it. It leapt into the waterhole, which is more than fifty yards wide.

When it was halfway across, I swung up the rifle and was about to fire when Tajurra stopped me and said, "Alligator."

The "alligator" was one which had taken quite a few head of our stock. It came behind the dingo, which had almost reached the opposite bank. The huge brute made its rush, jaws wide open, and snapped! The dingo yelped briefly, and then disappeared below in the jaws of the crocodile.

We had killed two pests and saved a calf for the cost of two bullets. But I still had not seen any pigeons. I said to Tajurra, "You want come catch pigeon?"

"All right," he said. "Plenty pigeon longa Two Mile Scrub. Me see plenty honey ant longa that place. You get pigeon, me get honey ant."

We set off at a canter for the Two Mile Scrub, which is a couple of hundred acres of rain forest down in a wide deep valley through which the creek flows.

On the way, Tajurra said, "Stop here, me show you honey ant longa nest."

We got down. He pulled a log away from the roots of a paperbark, and we knelt down to peer into the nest the log had been concealing. The worker ants were scurrying about on the floor.

The ceiling of the nest was formed by a mass of the paperbark's fine roots from which were suspended, by their jaws, the storage ants in their dozens, their stomachs the size of peas from the honey crammed into them by the working ants. Others were cramming them with still more honey they had been gathering from tree blossoms and wild flowers.

Tajurra put his hand into the nest and pulled out, one by one, a dozen or more of the distended ants from their anchorage. Putting them in the palm of his other hand, he offered them to me. I took them, somewhat gingerly, while he collected more for himself, which he immediately shoved into his mouth, heads and all.

"You no like sweet fella ant, Jimmy?" he asked.

"No more like head belonga him," I said. But I picked up one of the ants by its head and bit off its stomach. The taste was delightful, sweet yet sharp with the flavor of gum and wattle blossoms. I would have had more if it had not been for Tajurra telling me that the nest was his own particular "lolly" larder whenever he happened to be in the vicinity.

We rolled the log back into place and rode on over to the edge of the Two Mile Scrub, where we unsaddled the pony. I took the bit from its mouth and looped the reins around a fallen branch. The weight of the timber was enough to restrict the pony from wandering too far away. I left my high-heeled boots with the saddle.

We crossed over into the scrub. The descent down into the rain forest was an amazing experience: one moment we were in open grassy forest country, and the next we were being swallowed up by a jungle of gigantic trees lashed together in an almost impenetrable maze of huge vines, creepers, the massed growths of waitawhile lawyer canes, wild ginger, and a host of rampant undergrowth fighting upward for the sunlight.

Tajurra was able to find his way forward with an instinctive certainty of where he was going. He led the way down and along the valley floor toward the sound of cascading water until we came to Ebenezer's Waterfall, named after my grandfather.

A shallow wide stretch of boulder-strewn water at the foot of the fall is the one place where the creek can be crossed in safety without the danger of unseen crocodiles. But we were not the only ones to be at the waterfall that morning. A dozen women and girls from the camp were frolicking and laughing in the shallow water. Their coolamons, filled up with crocodile eggs, yams, and an assortment of mussels and mullee grubs, were lying on the ground.

When the women and girls spotted us, they

shrieked in merriment, "Tajurra! Jimmy! Come longa water!"

Tajurra and I sat down, and he shouted back, "What for you want me jump longa water longa woman? Me plurry man!" He pointed his finger at himself and the cicatrices on his arms and chest to prove it.

His action and his boast only served to send the women and girls into more laughter and giggling.

Tajurra made a downward motion of his hand to show his irritation at their antics; then he said to me, "No more get him pigeon longa this place, Jimmy; plurry women make noise altogether too much. Pigeon no come longa this fella tree." He pointed up into the branches of the tree behind us, a tall fig tree whose little figs lay scattered around us on the sand. The bronzewings love those figs and so do the wild pigs.

We got up and made our way across the shallow water. The giggling of the women and girls stopped, but it broke out again when we passed them to go between two huge boulders at the other side and on into the scrub.

We spent the better part of that day hunting around the scrub for the pigeons without any luck. However, in the afternoon Tajurra found some wild banana plants with a bunch of bananas ripening on them.

We cut the stalk down and carried it back to the sand under the fig tree by the waterfall and ate the bananas. The women and girls had gone. Tajurra and I were sitting quietly when he whispered, "Pigeon come."

I listened. The birds were up in the fig tree, feeding. I could see two of them. I aimed the rifle. Two quick shots got two plump pigeons. They fell behind the tree onto the narrow track that runs up the bank into the open forest. Tajurra went and picked up the dead birds, then he said, "Grandfather belonga you die near this fella tree, Jimmy."

"How you know that?" I asked.

"Tajalli tell it me. Tajalli find him dead longa pellet belonga shotgun."

"Who shoot 'im?" I asked, not knowing at that time how my grandfather had died.

"Nobody shoot 'im," Tajurra said. "Grandfather belonga you make trap longside this fella tree longa shotgun, shoot 'im pig. Pig come longa creek that side." He pointed to where the wild pigs come between the two boulders to cross over the shallow water to feed on the figs lying on the ground about us. He went on, "Pig no see string longa shotgun; pig hit 'im string, make gun fire, kill 'im pig."

"How grandfather belonga me die?" I asked.

"Tajalli say grandfather belonga you make trap longside this fella tree, go Walkabout longa other side; him come back by and by, forget trap here, him touch string longa gun; gun fire longa head longa grandfather. Him die finish."

And that is precisely how my grandfather died— by stumbling into his own trap when he bent down in the undergrowth and accidently touched the tight concealed cord tied from the tree to the trigger of the gun mounted halfway along the track leading up past the fig tree.

I tied the legs of the pigeons together for easier carrying and followed Tajurra onto the path alongside the fig tree. We stopped at the tree, and he showed me where some of the shotgun pellets had hit it. The raised marks, where the pellets had penetrated the bark, were clearly visible.

We went on up and out of the scrub and saddled up the pony. When I was slipping my boots back on, Tajurra said, "You like see Tajalli make big fella rain come by and by, Jimmy?"

"You tell the truth?" I asked, thinking he was joking because I didn't really believe in what he was telling me, even though Tajalli himself had said he would make the rain come after he and the Oonas went on their Walkabout.

"No tell lie," he answered. "When Tajalli sing longa stone and little fella turtle he got longa bag, by and by rain come quick smart, maybe three, four day."

"All right," I said, "When he do this fella song, make it rain?"

"Soon when sun go down in trees longa that place." He pointed to where the late afternoon sun was already sinking toward the treetops in the west. "Better we hurry."

We hopped up onto the pony and cantered back to the camp with the pigeons and rifle slung across my shoulder.

Tajalli and Nimapadi were standing under the pandanus palms, looking up at the sky over the Coral Sea.

Tajurra got down from behind me and said to Tajalli, "Jimmy want see you sing longa stone, longa turtle, make rain come."

Tajalli looked up at me on the pony and then at Nimapadi before he turned to me and said, "You make fool of me, Jimmy?"

"No make you fool," I answered. "Me think maybe you no want make rain come; maybe rain no more want come longa this place. Maybe you no want me see what you do. Maybe you think I tell everybody 'bout this. Me no do silly thing, Tajalli. Me no tell anybody. Why you no make rain come now?"

"This time altogether bad time," he explained and pointed out over the sea to the sky in the distance. Not a cloud was to be seen. "Sky tell me," he went on, "no more sing longa stone, longa turtle now. Sky say sing longa morning. You want see me do it sing, you come here longa morning. Me fix it by and by longa morning."

He and Nimapadi turned and walked into the camp.

"You come here longa morning?" Tajurra asked. "All Oona people go Walkabout longa morning, Jimmy."

"All right, I come here longa morning. 'Bye."

" 'Bye."

I rode home with the pigeons.

SIX

THE WET still hadn't arrived by the end of February, and my father was seriously concerned. Usually we could expect it fairly soon after the end of January. As elsewhere on the Peninsula, life on Oonaderra is governed by two seasons: the Wet and the Dry. Too long a Dry and the pastures—native grasses—cannot recover from the stock grazing on them. So far, Oonaderra had not experienced a prolonged drought with the horror and stench of dead and dying animals.

A continuation of the Dry could bring financial disaster for my parents, which was why, on the morning after I brought the pigeons home, my mother and father and I were standing on the front veranda watching the sky.

"I don't like it," Dad said. "I don't like it at all. There's not a damn sign of rain. I measured the tank this morning—it's down to less than nine inches. There's only enough water in it to last us another week at the most."

The galvanized iron rainwater tank at the side of the house holds about ten thousand gallons, which runs into it from the roof. The occasional storm or rain we get during the Dry are usually sufficient to maintain the tank at full capacity.

"Don't worry, Jack," Mum said hopefully; "we've had it as dry as this before now. We'll manage somehow."

"I hope so," he answered. "I don't want to have to start carting water from the creek." He turned to me and said, "The boongs are going Walkabout today, aren't they, Jimmy?"

"Yes, Dad."

"Has old Charley said anything about expecting rain?"

"Yes, he told me yesterday he was going to sing the rain this morning. He's going to try and make it come in a few days."

"Holy smoke! Has he got you believing in that damned rubbish? What I want to know is, Does he expect rain or not?"

"I don't know, Dad. He just said he would know this morning."

"Well, I know it's all a heap of stupid superstition," he answered. "But maybe Charley can tell what the weather is going to do. Are you going over there this morning?"

"Yes, Dad."

"All right then, ask him what he thinks about our chances of getting rain. And by the way, what's the idea of that cord you were wearing round your head yesterday?"

"Oh, Tajurra and I were acting the goat. I forgot I had the cord on when I came home."

He turned to Mum and said, "He's getting more like a boong every day. He's getting to be a savage."

"Oh, Jack! He's only having fun. What else can he do here?"

"Fun or no fun, he should have been sent to boarding school years ago; but you wouldn't have it. I just hope it's not too late for boarding school to lick him into shape. He certainly needs it."

Mum didn't answer, probably because my father was right—I should have been sent to school earlier. As it was, I did need civilizing—I thought and acted almost as an Aborigine.

"Well you had better get going," Dad said to me. "And don't forget to ask Charley what he thinks about our chances of getting rain."

"OK." I hopped over the veranda rail and was halfway down to the beach when he called out, "Hey, Jimmy!"

I stopped. "Yes?"

"And remind him to send those clothes and boots back to the saddle shed! And I want that snake's skin, too!"

"OK!" I was off like a shot before he could give me any further instructions.

Tajalli, Nimapadi, and Tajurra were under the pandanus palms on the beach when I arrived.

The two men and Tajurra were kneeling on the sand. In front of Tajalli was a short stick standing upright in the sand with a strip of red flannel tied to the top of it. The flannel was blowing and fluttering in the breeze coming from the southeast. To one side of the stick was a small heap of dry mangrove leaves and twigs, and alongside it lay a firestick, a piece of milky pine with a hole in it, and a tuft of dried swamp reed. On Tajalli's lap was his woven string bag. Because I was considered a brother of Tajurra, the bag was no longer taboo for me to see. I knelt beside Tajurra.

The three of them were watching the red flannel pennant fluttering in the breeze from the southeast. No one spoke. Now and then a lull in the breeze would cause the two men to take a deep breath, and they would lean forward expectantly. But the red rag would

86

drop and quickly lift again as the breeze freshened in from the same quarter.

This went on for ten minutes or so.

Then Tajalli bent forward. The breeze had stopped. For a moment or two the pennant hung limp. Tajalli tensed and looked out over the sea. Then he held out his hands before him, palms upward, and began in a cupping motion to draw the wind to himself. All the while he was whispering to the rain god, "Tirjila! Tirjila! Tirjila!"

Suddenly the red pennant lifted. The breeze had swung round and was coming in from the northeast over the Coral Sea. The piece of red flannel began to flutter madly in the wind.

Tajalli seized the firestick and commenced to twirl it in the hole in the piece of milky pine while Nimapadi thrust the tuft of dried swamp reed down the spinning point of the firestick. Tajalli kept repeating his whispered exhortation to "Tirjila! Tirjila! Tirjila!" until the edge of the hole in the piece of pine smoked and kindled into a glowing spark. He dropped the firestick, picked up the smoldering piece of pine and the dry tuft of reed in his cupped hands, and putting them to his mouth, began to blow on them. The tuft caught alight. He at once pushed it under the heap of leaves and twigs and commenced to chant, "Tirjila! Tirjila! Myee Oona! Tirjila! Tirjila!" The leaves and twigs blazed up in crackling orange and purple flames and were devoured in moments to a heap of white ash.

He stopped chanting to Tirjila and pulled up the stick with the red flannel on it. With it he leveled out the white ash and then carefully and slowly shaped it into a turtle with the head pointing into the northeast wind. Then he pushed the stick back into the sand and picked up the woven bag on his lap.

He opened it and tipped out the teji stones, "cat's-eyes," the mummified baby turtle, the bandicoot's skull, and the assortment of dried lizards onto the sand between his knees.

Nimapadi craned over to see in what pattern the bag's contents had fallen. Tajurra and I craned over, too. To me, the things lying there on the sand between Tajalli's knees meant nothing but a random collection of meaningless objects. But to Tajalli and Nimapadi the pattern they formed was a revelation because they both exclaimed excitedly, "Myee Oona!"

Tajalli scooped up his things and stowed them back in the bag.

I couldn't wait any longer to know why the mysterious ritual had been carried out so I asked, "Why do you do all this, Tajalli? How does this little fella rag, little fella fire tell you all about when rain come?"

He smiled, pointed out to sea, and said, "Little fella wind come longa that place; him tell me make fire make turtle longa ash; make all the things longa bag tell truth. Little fella turtle look first longa little fella wind. Turtle head look longa that place," and he pointed out to sea to the northeast to show how the turtle's head had faced that direction to indicate a favorable omen.

"Him tell you another fella wind come like a cyclone?" I asked.

Both men nodded vigorously, and Nimapadi said, "Him speak truth Jimmy—by and by, big fella wind come longa this place. Turtle no tell lie. Him tell truth."

Tajurra said to Tajalli, "How you know another little fella wind come longa this place this morning?"

"Sky tell it me last night," Tajalli answered. "Him say sing longa this place this fella morning."

I asked, "When will this big wind come?"

Tajalli promptly answered, "Three more day. Big fella wind come in nighttime. Him make too much rain altogether; make flood longa this place. Three more day."

We all stood up, and I said to Tajalli, "Father belonga me want know about rain. I tell him maybe rain come three more day?"

"No more!" Tajalli snapped impatiently. "You tell father rain come in three more day, longa nighttime."

I told him I was not doubting his word; I was only making sure that I was allowing for a possible variation in the time of the rain's arrival. But he was adamant—the rain would definitely arrive in three more days and at nighttime.

I accepted his word and then mentioned about the clothing and boots being sent back to the saddle shed.

He answered testily, "Woman wash clothes. She take it longa shed when dry."

The snake's skin? For me to ask about the return of the clothes and the snake's skin seemed a humiliating task. The fact that the clothing was already washed and would be sent back when it was dry was proof enough that they would be returned. In any case, white man's clothing and boots would have been utterly ridiculous for the Oonas to take on their Walkabout. Tajalli said, "You take Tajurra help you carry skin belonga that snake, Jimmy."

"All right."

I hated the thought of parting on bad terms with the Oonas. But I was quickly reassured when Tajalli kindly placed his hand on my shoulder and said, "No worry about father belonga you, Jimmy, telling you what you do; you no more cheeky boy—you the same as son belonga me. Me no feel mad longa you."

He and Nimapadi left us and strode away into the camp.

Tajurra heaved a sigh of relief and said, "Me think Tajalli get mad longa you; plenty time he get mad longa me, too. Him speak longa you the same as me."

"Better we get skin, Tajurra," I said, to save him

having to apologize for his father's attitude which was no more reprehensible than my own father's attitude toward me. We went to get the skin.

There was the washing as Tajalli had said: a dozen pairs of khaki pants and shirts were strung along on bushes and tree limbs to dry outside the camp as we passed on our way up to the timber to get the snake's skin.

Tajurra and I pulled the pegging stones away from it and turned the skin over to get the caked mixture of salty mud, shredded mangrove bark, and wood ash off it. Then the two of us walked up and down the skin half a dozen times to loosen and free it from the mixture. After that we rolled it up like a carpet and carried it over the rise to the saddle shed where Dad was working.

"Ah, hello, Titch," he greeted Tajurra as we walked in and put the skin on the big table.

" 'Lo, Boss."

"You big fella now, Titch, eh?"

"Yes, Boss. Me same as man now." He pointed proudly to his cicatrices to prove it.

"What for you get all the cuts longa you?" Dad asked. "Mad silly fella get cut all same as bullock get it brand longa bum. That silly stuff, make you same as bullock!" Dad laughed raucously. I felt a hot flush of shame come over me. Tajurra never said another word; he just walked outside to wait for me. My father was still chuckling to himself over his own tactless joke.

For the life of me, I could not see why he should speak in such a way when his own arms and chest were marked by half a dozen tattoos; and even my mother's ears had been pierced for earrings.

"Put that skin in the salt bin, Jimmy," Dad said, "and shove a few lumps on top of it."

"OK."

I put the skin in the bin. Then two of the men from the camp arrived with the clothes and boots.

"Hello, Bongo; hello, Jackie," Dad greeted them.

" 'Lo, Boss. We bring all the shirts, pants, and boots."

"All right, put them there." They stacked the clothes and boots behind the saddle rails and came over to Dad and me.

"When you go Walkabout?" Dad asked.

"By and by, Boss, when sun come up top," Jackie answered and pointed up to mid heaven. "You no more want us, Boss?"

"No, go on; clear out the pair of you."

They left, and Dad asked me what Tajalli had said about the likelihood of rain. I told him he had said the rain would come in three more days.

"Well, he'd better be right," he answered, "or I'll have the hide off him when he comes back from Walkabout if he's lying."

The amazing thing was that Dad dismissed all tribal lore as "Abo superstition," yet pinned his faith to Tajalli as a rainmaker. I was scared that Tajalli might be wrong in his forecast.

I left the shed, and Tajurra and I made for the camp while the going was good.

We went to the long mia-mia of the single men, and Tajurra showed me his newly made woomera and his long single-pronged hunting spear and triple-pronged fishing spear that he was now entitled to take on the Walkabout.

The other recently initiated young men were sitting around laughing and talking excitedly about the coming Walkabout. Tajurra and I joined in their chattering and joking. But after a while, Tajurra became quiet. He and I got up and wandered around the camp to watch the women preparing for the journey. Blankets, coolamons, and billies were stacked in heaps outside each mia-mia. Men, women, and children were going from group to group checking on the arrangements and order of marching that had to be followed according to tribal custom.

At the beach end of the camp, we watched Tajalli supervising the lifting of the dugout canoe from the creek for storing while they were away. Four men carried the canoe with the paddles in it up through the timber to the back of the camp. There they hoisted it into the parallel forks of two adjacent trees, well out of reach of floodwater or the possibility of fire.

Although Tajurra and I were watching all this commotion and activity, we were, at the same time, keenly aware of the parting to come between us. And both of us were incapable of voicing our feelings.

It was Tajalli who finally bridged the silence between us. Tajurra and I had talked of everything else while we wandered about the camp. Everybody was ready to leave. The whole tribe was assembled on the beach, Tajurra was beside me with his spears and woomera in his hand. The women were loaded with their camping gear. Some of the men were carrying the smaller children.

Tajalli, with shield in one hand and spears in the other, came up to us and said, "Maybe we no more see you for long time, Jimmy. When you come back longa Oonaderra?" I told him I would be coming home for the Christmas holidays. He was pleased and said, "Mind you no forget Oona people, Jimmy. Oona people no forget you. You all the same my people; all the same son belonga me; all the same brother belonga Tajurra. Me go now."

He looked intently at me; then, hesitantly, he rested his shield on the ground and awkwardly held out his hand.

"Good-bye, Jimmy."

"Good-bye, Tajalli." Our hands touched. Without another word he turned and walked to the edge of the creek.

Tajurra's hand and mine clasped tight. "Good-bye, Tajurra."

"Good-bye, Jimmy."

Then he strode over to his father and Nimapadi who were waiting for him. The three of them stepped into the creek and began crossing to the other side. The water was barely up to their lap-laps. The level had fallen more than two feet over the past few days.

The other men with their spears and woomeras crossed next, some of them carrying the smaller children. The bigger children crossed by themselves. Finally the women with their loads crossed and behind them swam the camp dogs.

Not once did the Oona people look back.

I watched them move in their easy loping gait perfected over the centuries to enable them daily to cover amazing distances. Within minutes they had rounded Rocky Point and vanished.

Suddenly the emptiness, the loneliness of the deserted camp, and the timeless quiet of Oonaderra overwhelmed me: I sat under the pandanus palms and cried till I could cry no more. I then bathed my face in the creek and went home.

For the next three days the wind from the northeast drove the temperatures up over the century mark in an intolerable heat wave of haze and burning sunlight, followed by nights of sweating and restless tossing on bedclothes hot from the heat locked in under the iron roof of the house.

On the afternoon of the third day my father decided to put a torch to the camp. It was necessary to burn it down to ensure that Tajalli's people would again use the site to rebuild their mia-mias, on return from Walkabout. If the mia-mias had been left standing the tribe would not have gone near them for fear of debbil-debbils which might be occupying them. But there was also another reason for its destruction: the fleas. The ground becomes impregnated with the pests from the camp dogs, and the only effective way to control them is literally to scorch the earth and destroy them by fire. The fleas were also one of the reasons why my father would never allow me to take Trudy near the camp.

In case the fire got out of control, we were armed with flails—wet bags tied to the ends of long poles—to fight it.

We first burned a firebreak around the dry grass surrounding the whole camp, except for the creek side. While Dad cautiously lit the rubbish with a torch of grass, a little at a time, I followed, belting out the flames that wanted to spread back into the timber from the northeaster blowing through the camp.

Yard by yard we burned back a wide swathe right down to the pandanus palms. We paused for a while to survey along the break to make sure that no fallen branches or logs had caught alight. It was all clear.

"Ready, Jim?" my father said with the flaming torch in his hand.

"OK, Dad. Let her go!"

He walked over to Tajalli's mia-mia and thrust the torch in through the low opening and stepped back out of range.

First, a wisp of blue smoke seeped up through the tinder-dry thatch. The next moment the mia-mia exploded in a roaring blaze of flames and sparks. In an instant the flames swept across to the adjoining mia-mias and raced through the camp.

"Run, Jimmy! Get round to the back in case she jumps the break!"

I raced up there with Dad after me. We stood back as the blazing wall of flames came traveling along like a tidal wave.

It reached the long mia-mia and engulfed it in one last great burst of fire before dying out completely.

Where the camp had stood was now only a wilderness of smoke-blackened trees and wisps of blue smoke curling up from the desolation of embers and ashes.

We checked through the site and put out all the fragments of smoldering timber that could ignite in the hot breeze.

"Well, that's that," Dad remarked with satisfaction. Then he said, "The water's a bit low in the house, so what about we peel off and have a bogey in the creek, eh?"

"OK."

He stripped to his blue-striped underpants; I took off my shirt, keeping my shorts on, and raced him to the creek.

We swam around in the warm water for a few minutes. When we came out, he spotted the nearly healed cicatrix on my arm.

"How the hell did you get that?" he asked.

"Aw, I caught my arm against the boiler the other day, Dad."

He looked intently at the scar and at me, but made no further comment. We gathered up our things and went home.

To say my father was worried about the nonarrival of the Wet would be to put it mildly. He was in a furious temper by the end of dinner that night. And the intolerable heat made matters worse; it was too hot even to go into the sitting room and sit on the big gray-and-pink-striped easy chairs. We sat instead in the canvas deck chairs on the front veranda, looking at the cloudless starry sky. Dad sat between Mum and me and continued his tirade against God, the weather, and all "the damn things a cattleman has to put up with."

"It's no use getting yourself all worked up, Jack," Mum said. "We'll just have to put up with things till the weather changes. This heat can't go on like this and not bring at least a storm to cool things down. Just relax and enjoy your pipe."

"I wouldn't give a tinker's damn," he answered, "if there was just the smallest sign to show that we could expect rain before that blasted tank runs dry. I wouldn't be a bit surprised if we miss out on the Wet altogether this year."

"But, Dad," I chipped in, "I told you Tajalli said the rain was sure to come."

"Did you now? And where is it? That Abo was lying as he and the rest of them always do when you ask them straight out about anything. My father always told me never to trust a burrie because he'll tell you exactly what he thinks you would like to know. And by God, my father was right! The things I've had to put up with from that thieving, lying mob of boongs would make any man want to belt into the swine and make 'em tell the truth."

"But, Dad," I persisted, "there's still plenty of time; Tajalli said the wind would come first at nighttime and the rain would follow it. It's still only eight o'clock."

"Well, my smart young weather prophet," he snapped back at me, "we'll see! Take a look out there —there is neither cloud nor wind in that sky. And I'll eat my damned hat if we get even a decent breeze before morning."

We went to bed by ten o'clock. I lay there in the stifling heat in my room listening to the grandfather clock whirring and striking each quarter hour and hour until I dozed off just after midnight.

Suddenly I was awakened. A wind had sprung up from the northeast and had begun to moan in gusts around the eaves of the house. I got up and looked through the window. There wasn't a star left in the sky.

My father had woken, too. He came round to my room in his blue flannel dressing gown. "Come on!" he shouted. "There's a big blow heading this way. Get all the stuff off the verandas into the lounge. Come on! Hurry!"

We dragged the things inside. Mum in her bright yellow nightgown was racing around closing every door and window. There was just a few minutes' grace left us after we had everything safely behind doors and windows. Then we sat down in the furniture-piled sitting room to wait.

Suddenly Dad said, "Listen."

Coming in over the Coral Sea was the screaming sound of an approaching cyclone. In a matter of seconds it reached the house in a roaring crescendo that made the walls bulge inward under the terrific strain. Then the rain! It came down in a fury as though the heavens and the wind were hell-bent on annihilating us. The wind eased slightly, but the roaring downpour continued. I went over to the thermometer hanging on the wall above the gramophone cabinet. The temperature had dropped from above the century to sixty degrees in less than five minutes!

"Well, we'd better all get to bed," Mum said. Sleep came easily to us with the sound of the rain drumming endlessly on the roof. . . .

In the morning, just as Tajalli had said, the creek was running a banker and spreading out over the land on either side.

That Wet lasted for two months before it began to ease toward the end of April, two months in which my correspondence lessons became the one thing my mother and I had to distract us against the boredom of that interminable rain. We had no wireless. Dad said there was no reception at all on Oonaderra, and he wouldn't have a wireless, anyway. He preferred to keep the outside world away; he read.

The thought of leaving Oonaderra for school became less frightening to me. Being cooped up by the Wet made going to the Outside seem like a great adventure.

SEVEN

UP TO the last moment before my departure from Oonaderra I had not realized that I was being literally torn by the roots from the only world I knew. Despite the future that was being planned for me, I was as inseparably linked to the fate of Oonaderra as were my own family and the Oona people. Yet fate, it would seem, had given me a choice: I was leaving this place, and there was no reason why I should return to live here permanently.

By daybreak on the morning of my departure my father had been over in the home paddock saddling up eight packhorses in readiness; he was making the trip to Cairns coincide with his usual four-monthly journey to bring back supplies. He brought his big chestnut and a big silver bay for me over to the house and hitched them to the back veranda rail.

Breakfast was over. My mother came out to the veranda with us to say good-bye. She hugged and kissed Dad and told him to be careful. He promised he would and climbed up into the saddle. "See you over at the saddle shed, Jim," he said to me, and swung his horse around to ride slowly across to the rise. He was giving Mum and me the chance to say good-bye alone.

"Oh, Jimmy, Jimmy. My poor little Jimmy." In a moment she had let the held-back emotion of my leaving her come to the surface. She held me in her arms with all her love and fierce reluctance to let me go. "You will write every week, won't you, dear?"

"Yes, Mum. I promise."

"Anyway, you'll be home for Christmas, and then we'll make up for everything, eh?"

"Yes, Mum." I walked out to the silver bay and jumped up into the saddle. "Good-bye, Mum."

She whispered her "Good-bye" because she had lifted the hem of her apron to hide the tears.

I turned the horse and rode up to the top of the rise where I pulled up for one last look at her standing and waving to me. I waved back. The sun was just rising out of the sea, and the long, low silhouette of the colonial house stood out with its sprawling low-pitched iron roof and rounded overhang above the verandas. It and my mother made a sharply etched picture that I was to remember always when the loneliness of crowds and other different buildings swamped me.

I rode down to my father waiting at the saddle shed with the halter rope of the leading packhorse ready in his hand.

"OK, Jim?"

"OK, Dad."

He dug his heels into the chestnut's flanks and set off with me in the rear of the packhorse line heading west and south to avoid the river and creek mouths. The deep water after the Wet would mean swimming the horses across them.

100

It was the tail end of the Wet, and the grass and surface water were in abundance, so the horses were assured of easy pickings and good water. We were making south for Mount Molloy, two hundred miles away.

Hour after hour Dad kept the team moving at a steady pace. Not until one o'clock did he halt to rest the horses past the hottest part of the day, and for us to boil the billy and eat the sandwiches Mum had prepared. Not once had he allowed the horses to drink at any waterhole or creek we crossed; he had to prevent them from distending themselves while they were overheated and soft from lack of work.

At three o'clock we were on our way again, and it was after nightfall before we reached the point Dad was making for to camp and hobble out the horses by the edge of a shallow billabong.

We got a fire going, and in no time at all Dad had spuds and onions cooking in a billy and another one on the fire for tea. We had the vegetables with slabs of cold corned beef and bread on tin plates, and washed the meal down with pannikins of hot tea. It was surprising just what could be done with a couple of billycans and a frying pan.

Afterward we lay back on our bedding rolls while Dad filled and lit his pipe with a glowing stick from the fire.

"How you feeling, Jim?" he asked.

"A bit homesick. And I'm a bit worried about Mum being left alone."

"Aw, don't worry, son; Mum will be all right—she knows how to look after herself. And it's only natural that you would be feeling a bit homesick. But you'll soon get over that once you meet Mum's mother and father down in Brisbane. They're a nice old couple, and you'll enjoy staying with them overnight. They'll take you over to the school and introduce you to the headmaster. You'll get into the swing

101

of things in no time at all. I did, when I was down there at school. I was one of the first pupils when it opened in 1918. Had a marvelous time at old 'Churchie.' I was sorry when I had to leave, I can tell you. Had the best time of my life there."

"Then why did you leave Brisbane, Dad?"

"Had to come back to Oonaderra to take over when my mother and father died in 1920."

He said "died" rather than state outright the violent manner in which his parents had met their deaths.

"And you lived by yourself on the property for a long time, didn't you?" I asked.

"Yes, until I met your mother on a trip I made to Brisbane."

"Did she like the idea of living out in the back-blocks, Dad?"

"Oh, she didn't mind. But when you came along that clinched it; you became her pride and joy, and from then on she didn't mind at all about having to live on Oonaderra. And that made me feel good, too. Couldn't imagine myself being without her now. As a matter of fact, I'm not too happy about losing you, Jim."

"Well," I answered like a shot, "you don't have to. We could call the whole thing off if you're willing! I am!"

"Yes, Jim. I know. But that wouldn't be the right thing to do at all. It's like I told you before—you've got to learn to mix with white people; you've got to get an education. If you don't, you'll regret it for the rest of your life. And, as I told you before, you'll want to meet girls, and no doubt marry one day. But first you've got to find out what it is you want to do with your life. Have you given it any thought, yet?"

"No; I would rather be a cattleman than anything else."

"Well, there's no reason why you can't be one

day. And remember, even a cattleman has to have an education to handle a property these days; he's got to be accountant, manager and every other thing you can think of if he's going to make a go of it. So you get stuck into getting yourself educated, my boy, and later on you'll probably end up with exactly what you want. Mark my words."

"Yes, I will."

"Well, we've another long haul tomorrow, so I reckon we'd better hit the sack, eh?"

"Yes, Dad."

We unrolled our groundsheets and blankets side by side. He put a couple of logs on the fire; then we took off our shoes and hats, placed them at the foot of our bedding, lay down, and pulled the blankets up over our shoulders.

"Good night, Jim."

"Good night, Dad."

He was asleep in moments. I lay for a long while looking at the fire glowing red in the soft night wind. All the sounds of the bush, which would have normally lulled me off, kept me awake thinking of home and what it really would be like once my father said good-bye.

I remember the crescent-shaped waning moon coming through the shadows of the trees and the mournful calls of curlews in the distance, and I closed my eyes. . . .

It seemed but a few moments had passed when Dad shook me. "Come on, Jim, breakfast."

I went and sluiced my hands and face in the billabong and came back to the crackling fire on which Dad was serving from the frying pan thick slices of rusty bacon and pufftaloons onto our plates. He had a billy of tea ready with the pannikins.

"Feel like eating?" he asked.

"You bet."

We set to and finished off our breakfast. Then

he said, "You clean up the things and pack them. I'll saddle up and we'll get going before sunup."

"Right you are."

Within fifteen minutes we were on our way, just as the sun was coming up through the timber over on our left.

Dad unerringly headed for the camp sites he had used so often on his trips to and from Mount Molloy. The sites were fairly equal distances apart and situated where he knew there would be shade and water to break the daily average of miles covered. I knew he was also wanting to get back home to Mum in the shortest possible time.

It took us five days to reach Mount Molloy and Carl Muller's place, on the outskirts, where we unsaddled the horses and let them go. They were fenced in and safe. Carl Muller was the local carrier for the surrounding area and every weekday he made the fifty-odd-mile journey to Cairns and back in his huge truck. Dad always went into Cairns with Carl for supplies and to attend to other matters at his bank and with the solicitor who handled all his legal affairs. Later Carl would collect the orders, and he and Dad would return to Mount Molloy with them.

We piled the saddles in Carl's big shed and went over to his unpainted weatherboard house, which was open for all visitors to drop in and wait if he were absent. He wasn't there when we arrived, but we didn't have to wait long before his huge truck came rumbling up to the house and all sixteen stone of him came bouncing inside. Dad and I were seated on two of the half-dozen camp stretchers in the one big room.

"Well, stone the bloody crows!" he greeted us. "I didn't expect you for another fortnight, Jack!"

"Had to bring the lad along, Carl," Dad answered. "He's going down to Brisbane to go to 'Churchie'; thought I might as well get my business done in Cairns at the same time."

104

"Yair. No sense in making two trips." And turning to me, he said, "Last time I saw you, Jimmy, must have been all of six years ago." To my father he said, "You've got a fine lad there, Jack. What's he going in for?"

"Not sure yet, Carl. We'll see what he thinks after he's had a couple of years at school."

"Yair. Well, I always say, don't push 'em; let 'em decide for themselves what they want to be. That way they can't come back at you if they make a mess of things; not that I think Jimmy ever would, but you never can tell with the way the world and the kids in it are acting these days. Every bloody thing's flamin' madness, and kids are growing up with all the wrong ideas. You mark my words, Jack, the next generation isn't going to cop the things we copped in our young days. Ah, well, how about we get ourselves a feed, eh?"

We all pitched in, and it helped to keep my self-pity at a safe distance from the eyes of the men.

The next day we set off in Carl's truck for Cairns where my father first took me to buy a new gray suit and blue shirt. Then he brought me a new suitcase and the things I would need as a boarder at "Churchie."

But the city, the traffic, and the streets swarming with people overwhelmed me. For me, a boy totally unaccustomed to civilization, it was all so strange. The peace and calm of Oonaderra were something I would have raced back to if I could. No school was going to hold me against my will. I would invent some reason so that even my father would allow me to return home. It was this thought that saved me from despair.

Then the railway station. My father carrying my suitcase and putting it up on the rack and sitting down on the seat to give me his last-minute instructions and advice, "Now, remember, Jim, when you reach Brisbane, don't leave the platform until you're met by Mum's parents. They'll be on the lookout for you, and they'll know you by the clothes you're wearing. Mum sent them a letter a couple of months ago. They will put you up at their place until you go to school. I've arranged for the school to buy you anything else you need. And you'll get five shillings a week pocket money. And take this for your journey." He gave me five one-pound notes.

Handling money bewildered me. I had never bought a thing in my life. The value of it meant nothing. I had not the faintest notion of how to go about buying something. But my father assumed that there would be no difficulty for me in that direction.

How little he really knew of what I was feeling, yet I know now he was doing in his own laconic Australian way the very best he could.

"Now look, Jim," he said, "stuff that money in your pocket and don't go flashing it around, or you might get yourself a belt over the head and be robbed."

I nodded and stuffed the notes into my trousers pocket. Then the passengers began swarming into the train.

"Well, Jim." Dad stood up. "Take care of yourself and don't forget to write. Your mother will never forgive you if you don't."

"I won't forget, Dad."

He held out his hand and shook mine; then he walked out onto the platform. I watched him waving self-consciously as the train began to pull out of the station. I waved back from my window seat and kept my face turned from the woman beside me. Fortunately I had a seat at the end of the carriage, separate from all the others. I began to cry.

Somehow I managed to get my handkerchief out of my pocket to my face.

"What's the matter, son?"

That voice, the gentle voice of that woman who sat beside me, sounded exactly like my mother's. I turned my streaming face to her.

"Leaving home for the first time?" she inquired kindly.

I nodded because my sobbing wouldn't let me speak.

"You know something?" she asked with the sweetest of smiles.

I shook my head.

"You're the image of my own son. And when I saw you crying just then, it all came back to me—he cried fit to break his heart when I saw him off to boarding school—exactly the same as you."

"Did he?" I asked, less ashamed now that I knew someone else had been in the same situation as myself.

"He certainly did," she assured me. "And what's more, he turned out to be the best rowing cox his school ever had. He's a scientist now. And I often tease him about the time he didn't want to leave me."

"Gee, maybe that's what I'll be one day," I said, my tears gone but still not far from starting again.

That woman saved me! On all that interminable thousand-mile journey she stood by me and guided me: in the dining car or on the drafty night stops in station refreshment rooms, she was always there beside me to see that I got proper food instead of the junk I wanted to buy.

She answered every one of my questions patiently and gently, and in the endless swaying and clicketing of the train in the long night hours, her shoulder was always there. She has no need of my blessing because, wherever she is now, she is sure to be receiving from others a full appreciation of her kindness of spirit.

Fate stood by me to the end of that thousand-mile journey and then delivered me into the arms of my white-haired grandparents, who swamped with love the grandson they had never before set eyes on.

Then I was whisked into a taxi and taken to their home, less than half a mile from "Churchie" where I was checked in the next day to begin my first term.

I survived the ordeal of initiation by the older established students; actually it was far less of an ordeal than the one Tajurra had endured to bring him into manhood. I learned to accept and to tolerate, even to enjoy myself.

But there were times when my longing and the homesickness for Oonaderra got me down, and it was then that I retreated to Grandma and Grandpa's place to recover myself.

EIGHT

MY FATHER left the letter writing to Mum, and she kept me informed of all that was happening at Oonaderra. In her first letter she said that the last mob of bullocks Dad had sent out were sold at record prices. She also hinted at a big surprise for me later on—if she could get round Dad now that he was in a better financial position.

In her next letter she told me she had succeeded: Dad had bought a thirty-five-foot, diesel-powered cabin cruiser—the *Curlew*—equipped with two-way radio!

She went on to say, "Think of it, Jimmy—I'll never be left alone again because I can now go to Cairns with Dad whenever we need supplies. Already I have made one trip with him; and, guess what, I can handle the *Curlew* all by myself! And when you break up for the Christmas holidays, we'll be able to pick you up in Cairns for the trip home. Isn't that wonderful and exciting?"

It was indeed! But it didn't alter the fact that I still had to face the rest of the school year before seeing the craft and being back on Oonaderra. In her next letter, my mother told me how they had solved the problem of getting their supplies up from the beach to the storeroom on the property. She said Dad had bought a big old-fashioned horse-drawn brewery dray in Cairns which had been converted from its original four wooden, iron-tired wheels to truck wheels with big balloon tires. She described how they had had to dismantle the whole thing to get it into the hold of the boat and then reassemble it back on the property. But it had all been worthwhile because the dray's low, flat top made loading and unloading fairly easy; and the wide rubber tires were just the thing for negotiating the sandy beach when Nellie, the draft horse, was hauling the supplies across it and up the road Dad had cut in the side of the slope leading to the storeroom.

At long last, term was ended and I was on my way home. I had passed my exams with reasonably good results. Grandma and Grandpa saw me off at the station.

That rail journey seemed longer than ever to me in my eagerness to see the *Curlew*. But it was soon forgotten when I eventually stood with Mum and Dad on the Cairns esplanade and he, proudly pointing to the *Curlew* out in the harbor, said, "Well, there she is. What do you think of her?"

I gasped at the sight of the beautiful boat with its trim, white hull and varnished superstructure shining on the bright blue water in the morning sunlight.

Mum squeezed my hand and said, "Come on, dear, let's get out there, and you can see for yourself just how lovely she really is."

Down the steps we clambered to our moored dinghy, and rowed out to the boat where we were greeted excitedly by Trudy and Suney, who loved traveling on the *Curlew*. I was shown the big diesel, the four-berth cabin, the wheelhouse, and, of course, the cabinet housing the two-way radio, operated either by batteries or, in an emergency, by pedal generator.

Under the forward hatch Dad showed me the hold filled with supplies for Oonaderra.

"Gosh," I said, "I never thought we'd own a boat, especially one like this."

"Neither did I, Jim. And if it hadn't been for the good prices we got for our last lot of bullocks and your mother talking me into buying the *Curlew* out of the proceeds, I would never have thought about it."

"But you're not sorry you did, are you?"

"Sorry! I'll say not! Why, I've never known such peace of mind as I've got now, knowing I'll never have to leave Mum on her own again. No, Jim, this is the best thing your mother and I ever decided on."

"I'm glad you did, Dad. When do we leave?"

"Just as soon as I winch up the anchor. Tell Mum to take over while I do it."

"OK."

Mum was in the galley, making morning tea. "Dad wants you to take over," I said, longing to see how she made out at the wheel.

"All right," she answered.

She went up to the wheelhouse, and climbed nonchalantly up into the swivel chair, took the wheel in one hand and with the other pressed the starter button; the motor purred into life.

Through the window Dad signaled to her, and like a veteran liner captain she manipulated the clutch and gear lever, and the craft swung slowly round and headed out to sea.

I could hardly believe the way she handled the boat with such ease and confidence. She laughed and said, "Well, was I right? Didn't I tell you everything had turned out to be so exciting?"

"Gosh, yes, Mum. But I never ever imagined

seeing you running a boat like this. How about letting me have a go, eh?"

"Here's Dad. Ask him."

He had no objections. Mum went back to the galley, and I took the wheel, Dad standing beside me to point out the landmarks to steer by, and telling me to memorize them because they were the only guides and beacons we had to rely on to keep us away from the coral reefs.

My father was never a man to take unnecessary risks, so, before sundown, he steered the *Curlew* into the lee of one of the small uninhabited islands dotted along the Cape York coastline and we dropped anchor for the night.

While Mum was preparing dinner, he and I went into the wheelhouse and sat by the radio. Before he switched on the set, he said, "By the way, Jim, you had better remember the routine of handling the radio in case you ever need to call the outside in an emergency. This is the dual transmitting and receiving switch—" he flicked it to the T and the R and back to Off—"and that's our identification call sign. It's not hard to operate; just switch to T and give the call sign over the microphone if ever you need help."

The call sign was printed along the base of the set: M. V. CURLEW: Q. EIGHT TWO ZERO.

He switched on the receiver. We listened to the news and the weather report which was "continuing fine along the coast from Cairns to Thursday Island." We left the set on to listen to music while we had dinner under the canopy.

What a perfect night it was. A brilliant moon was rising out of the sea, and in the soft breeze the coconut palms were swaying above the island's other vegetation.

In the morning Dad grilled fish steaks from a big Red Emperor he had caught while Mum and I were asleep. Immediately after breakfast we got under way again.

112

It was late afternoon when we arrived at the channel, the Oonas came onto the beach to wave us the helm. As he steered the *Curlew* through the channel, the Oonas came on to the beach to wave us a welcome home. We waved back, and Dad, now clear of the reef, swung the boat hard to port and continued on to the anchorage directly opposite the house. He was anxious to get the supplies ashore before dark.

He rowed us ashore with the dog and cat, all of us happy to be back home again. At the house, while Mum set about getting the stove going for dinner, Dad and I went over to the home paddock, he armed with half a loaf of stale bread to catch Nellie and harness her up to the dray parked outside the saddle shed.

With her bridle in one hand and the bread in the other, all Dad had to do was call, "Kip, kip, kip. Come on, old girl!" and Nellie came ambling up for the tasty tidbit which she got after the bit and bridle had been slipped over her head.

We harnessed her into the shafts and climbed aboard the first wheeled vehicle ever to roll over Oonaderra. For me it was a hilarious experience, at first, to sit beside Dad as he flicked the reins to get Nellie started with a "Giddup there, Nellie!" She set off for the beach with me bursting my sides laughing until Dad said dryly, "OK, my boy—let's see you laughing when we start manhandling those supplies ashore and up to the storeroom. You won't think it's funny then."

"OK, Dad," I answered, knowing that discretion would serve me better than to anger him when he was serious.

And a serious business it was, too, ferrying the stuff from the boat to the dray and from the dray to the storeroom. By then it was almost dark, so I had no chance of getting over to the camp to see Tajurra because the supplies had still to be sorted out before Dad would even think of knocking off.

If it had not been for the taboo which prevented the Oonas from setting foot across the invisible line of demarcation surrounding the house, how simple it would have been for all of us to meet without the tribe living in constant dread of incurring the vengeance of their god Oona if they stepped over into the forbidden territory.

And how much more comfortable it would have made the daily routine for my mother if she could have had men from the tribe to help out with her gardening; and how much more convenient it would have been for her to have trained a couple of the Aboriginal girls to help out in the kitchen and around the house. But the tradition had been established by my grandparents fifty years before that no Aborigine would ever be allowed near the house under any circumstances. My father continued the tradition even more vehemently than my grandparents.

The hidebound customs of a lifetime were too firmly established in the thinking of my parents, especially my father, for them to want to change them willingly through reason. And, of course, there was no hope for a change of attitude on either side of the black-white issue on Oonaderra—not while our house remained standing over the ancient, sacred Bora Ring of the Oona people.

Even as far as I was concerned, at that particular time, the Curse meant very little to me beyond the fact that I knew of it through Tajurra. In any case, I was home for one purpose only—to enjoy myself. But holiday or no holiday, there was still plenty of work to do around the property. My father saw to that.

He discussed with Mum and me that night the work he wanted to get done before the New Year. First, he wanted the fences inspected and repairs carried out where necessary; then the cattle had to be mustered and yarded for the branding of young stock and the dipping of the whole herd for tick infestation—

a necessity if the stock were to be kept in good condition, especially the bullocks he intended to cull out for sending to the sale yards before the Wet set in.

It had been an uncommonly dry year, with only occasional, light, patchy rain falling on Oonaderra since the last Wet, so I didn't pay very much attention to Dad's perennial complaint: "This damn year's worse than any I can remember for rain—we haven't had one decent storm to fill the house tank; and the feed on the property has just about had it. If we don't get a good soaking soon, we'll be in real trouble, I'm telling you. Anyway, I'll have to see how the cattle look before I can decide if it's worth sending a mob out."

Mum didn't look up from the doily she was crocheting. "When will you be going out to look at the fences?"

"Tomorrow. And you, Jimmy, go over and harness Nellie to the dray first thing in the morning before breakfast and load up the fencing gear ready for an early start. Then I want you to slip over to the camp and tell old Charley and Paddy I want them and a couple of the others for the fencing job. OK?"

"OK, Dad."

"Oh, by the way, Jack," Mum said, "when do you think Jimmy should go back to Brisbane?"

"It all depends on when the Wet starts," he answered. "We'll just have to get the weather reports over the radio, and if there seems to be any likelihood of a cyclone developing, we'll have to leave with him right away to get him out; otherwise, we can leave it to the last week in January before we make the trip to Cairns."

She nodded her agreement and went on crocheting.

Needless to say, I was all for no cyclone coming along to cut my holiday short, but I was careful not to say so openly; as far as Dad was concerned, he would have welcomed a cyclone right then and there if it meant getting the rain the property so desperately needed.

When I crossed over the rise to the saddle shed first thing the next morning, I was more observant than I had been the previous evening in my eagerness to see the dray. All around was proof of the urgent need for good rains soon. The native pasture grasses were already almost eaten down to ground level in the home paddock and were showing no resurgence of new growth. Such grasses need fairly regular rain, even in the Dry, when we could count on the occasional storm or showers to maintain feed for the stock, and water in the house and washhouse tanks.

With the aid of the bread I had brought, I had no trouble catching Nellie. I had just got the bridle on her when Tajurra came running over from the camp. "Jimmy! 'Lo, Jimmy!"

"Tajurra! Gee! How are you?"

In a moment we were grasping each other's hands in the excitement of our reunion.

He asked, "You like school, Jimmy?"

I pulled a face.

He grinned and said, "Maybe father, mother belonga you let you stop longa Oonaderra all the time now, eh?"

"No fear," I said. "Him tell me suppose cyclone come he take me away quick smart longa Cairns."

He nodded sadly at the prospect and then brightened up. "Tajalli think cyclone not come longa this place for long time; maybe no get Wet this time."

"What for he say that?" I asked.

He shrugged noncommittally. "Don't know. Him tell Nimapadi. Him say maybe by and by he make little fella fire, look longa things he got longa bag, ask longa wind send rain. Maybe by and by."

And that was all he could, or would, tell me about Tajalli's plan to invoke in the "by and by" the help of Tirjila, the god of the rains, to bring relief to drought-stricken Oonaderra.

116

He gave me a hand in harnessing Nellie to the dray, and I gave him the message for Tajalli to bring Nimapadi and a couple of others to help with the fence inspection and repairs.

And so, for the next few weeks, we were busy fence repairing, carting firewood in readiness for when the Wet would set in, and finally, the cattle were mustered and yarded, and the branding and dipping against ticks was carried out. The cattle, especially the mature bullocks that Dad had planned sending off to the sale yards, were not in very good condition, so he decided to hold them over until after the Wet to give them a spell on good feed.

All in all, it was a good Christmas. And, in the following week, Dad decided to slaughter a "scrubber"—a huge red bullock that had given us a lot of trouble during the mustering by repeatedly charging the men and horses. We needed fresh meat and corned beef for the brine cask in the storeroom.

The beast was shot over by the yards, and there was no shortage of helpers in the skinning and dressing when the Oonas were told that there was fresh bullock meat. They took the blood, the head, the entrails, and a hindquarter of the beast for their share. That night a feast and corroboree went on at the camp until the middle of the night.

At home we had plenty of roast beef as well as the brine cask filled to the brim with the remainder of the beast salted down. All we needed to end the year on a happy note was rain.

The New Year arrived but not the rain. Dad was getting desperate. Now that he had given us a respite from work, Tajurra and I rode over Oonaderra, and hunted wild pigs with Tajalli and the other men.

Then, about a week before I was due to go back to school, a fishing boat came through the reef during the night and anchored offshore up at Rocky Point. We were just about to sit down to breakfast when Dad came into the dining room carrying his binoculars. He said, "There's a Chinese fishing boat anchored off the point. The crew's ashore, and they've got fires going already. Must be trepangers." We ran out after him to the front veranda to see what was going on.

Through the glasses I saw the Chinese, dressed in straw hats, black knee-length pants and jumpers, stoking fires under big caldrons beside long wire-netting racks with fires smoking beneath them.

"What are they doing?" I asked.

Dad took the glasses, focused them on the men and answered, "Looks like they're curing trepang, sea slugs, or whatever it is you call them; beats me how the Chinese or anybody else can eat those things as a delicacy. I'd better go along there after breakfast to warn them to be careful with those damn fires or they're likely to burn out the property the way things are at the moment."

After breakfast I went with him. We had no trouble in crossing the creek where it flows onto the beach. The water was barely up to our ankles.

As we thought, the Chinese were trepang fishermen. They were dipping netting baskets of the fat sea slugs into the caldrons of boiling water before splitting them open and stacking them along the wire-netting racks to be dried and smoked. When Dad addressed the Chinese, they made a great pretence of "no saveeing" ("not knowing") what he was saying to them. They knew, of course, that they had no right to be ashore on the Australian mainland. To everything he said they just answered, "Whaffor? Whaffor?" or, "No savee. No savee."

Dad was about to turn away in anger when one of them, no doubt the skipper, who probably thought that he would get in touch with the authorities, came up and said, "All this man speak only Chinese, no understand—no speak English!"

Dad told him there was no need to be afraid; he

only wanted the men to be careful not to let their fires get away into the bush.

The man seemed immensely relieved. He assured Dad that such a thing would not happen. As a parting gesture of goodwill, he asked if we would like to take some of the trepang home. "Velly nice, eat with rice," he said, holding out a double handful of the squirming slugs for Dad to take.

Dad pulled a wry face, backed away, and declined with a hurried, "No thanks," and we left the Chinese to their work.

It didn't take the Oonas long to offer the Chinese their help in the hope of getting a share of the trepang, which they had always been rewarded with in former years by other fishermen who had used the point for their curing. They were not disappointed.

Every evening we rowed out to check on the *Curlew* and, of course, to tune in for the news and weather reports. A couple of evenings after the trepangers arrived on Oonaderra, Mum came with us to the boat, and we heard the weather report we had been hoping for: "An intense low-pressure system, developing out over the Coral Sea, is moving slowly toward the coast. Good rains are expected within the next few days, extending from the tip of Cape York Peninsula and along the entire coastal belt to Cairns and beyond."

"Thank God for that!" Dad said.

Mum and I smiled. At last the strain of waiting and watching the sky for storm clouds would soon be over. Poor Dad. At that time I was not able to fully appreciate what it meant to be a cattleman responsible for decisions that could mean the difference between economic security or possibly ruin and disaster.

My parents were in good spirits, but my heart sank when Dad said, "Well, Jim, my boy, we'll have to be getting you back to school. We'll have to leave in the morning."

"Oh, not tomorrow!" I pleaded and turned to my mother to enlist her aid. "Not tomorrow, Mum, please!"

"It's up to your father, Jimmy," she answered.

"Well?" I asked anxiously.

My father smiled and said, "Oh, all right. But, mind you—we can't leave it too long. Now let me see . . . today's Thursday . . . you can stay till Sunday morning. That's final."

"Gee, thanks!" I was determined to make the most of my last two days on Oonaderra. The next morning Tajurra and I saddled up a gray stock horse for him and Creamy for me, and we rode to all our favorite places on the property.

In the late afternoon we were on our way back to the home paddock. At the stockyards over by the lagoon, Tajurra pulled up and pointed. "Look!" A man was running and stumbling from the camp up the slope of the rise waving and brandishing a bottle, and some fifty yards behind, the Oonas were racing after him.

Tajurra gasped, "Nimapadi! Him drunk!"

Nimapadi reached the top of the slope, where the path leads down over the other side of the rise and across to the house. He paused for a moment and then disappeared down the path on the other side.

We dug our heels into the horses' flanks and galloped across and up to the top of the rise behind the shrieking Aborigines, who were shaking their fists at the drunken Nimapadi. He had raced to the house and was on the back veranda steps, shouting and waving the bottle at my parents, who were dumbfounded at the sight of him.

My father turned, walked into the house and came back carrying a double-barreled shotgun. He swung the gun up and aimed it directly at Nimapadi, who immediately dropped the bottle.

The tribe fell silent. I closed my eyes and waited for the shot to come.

Tajalli, who was standing in front of his people, shouted an order to them. I opened my eyes. The Oonas were running back along the top of the rise, leaving Tajurra and me sitting alone astride our ponies. Nimapadi, shocked by the sight of Dad's gun, had taken to his heels and was running like a madman toward the camp, with his hands clasped over his eyes to shut out the sight of the taboo ground he had trespassed on.

I looked at Tajurra. He was trembling, and his black face had gone gray with fear at the terrible thing Nimapadi had done. By flouting the Curse of Oona and the tribal taboo, he well knew it could mean the end for the Oonas. Before I could reason with him, Tajurra leapt from his saddle and said fearfully, "Altogether too many bad things come longa this place now, Jimmy. Better me go now." He handed me the reins of his pony and, without another word, ran down along the top of the rise after his people.

Knowing my father's temperament where the Aborigines were concerned, I realized that he, by a hair's breadth, had avoided a repetition of what his father had done half a century before in shooting down the leader of the Oonas. My father had enough trouble to contend with, without having the burden of murder on his conscience.

I took the horses over to the saddle shed, let them go, and went straight home. We found out later that the bottle Nimapadi had been drinking from was a gift from the Chinese—a bottle of their potent rice brandy for helping to cure the trepang. In the morning the Chinese were gone, leaving behind the tragic consequences of their stay on Oonaderra for others to face.

After breakfast I went along the beach to the camp to speak to Tajurra. He was sitting under the pandanus palms with the men of the tribe, but he would not leave the circle nor even speak to me when I called to him. Nor would any of the others speak to me except Tajalli who just said, "Better you go away, Jimmy."

It was useless trying to remonstrate, so I went back home.

The following day I boarded the *Curlew* with my parents for the trip to Cairns. As Dad was swinging the boat into the channel out to sea, I saw the Oonas standing under the palms. I waved good-bye to them. Only one hand waved back—dear Tajurra's! I knew he had gone against the tribe in doing so.

Ironically, after less than an hour's sailing, we were deluged with rain which did not let up all the way to Cairns. And it was still pouring when I waved good-bye to my parents from the train. I thought, What a blessing the arrival of the Wet would be for the whole of Oonaderra.

NINE

THE ARRIVAL of the Wet on Cape York Peninsula invariably puts an end to land travel between the properties and the people on them. Therefore, after my return to school, I did not expect to hear from home for some time because the mailman would not be able to get through. And I knew that it might be at least three months before my parents would sail to Cairns for more supplies.

But about a month later I was called to the headmaster's office. He said, "Brent, I've had a telephone call from your grandparents. They've asked me to excuse you from school for the rest of the day. They want you to go home right away."

"Why, what's the matter, Sir?" I was alarmed by his manner which told me something bad had happened.

"I think you had better hear the news from your grandparents," he answered. "Have you money for your tram fare?"

"Yes, Sir."

"Very well then, you get home as quickly as you can."

"Yes, Sir. Thank you, Sir."

Grandma and Grandpa were sitting on the sofa in the living room when I arrived. Grandma was crying.

"Come and sit here, dear," she said.

I sat between them.

Grandpa said, "Your mother has written to us, Jimmy, and put a letter for you in with ours so that we could break the news to you gently before you read it." Turning to Grandma, he said, "You tell him, dear."

She put her arm round me to comfort me and through her tears she said, "Jimmy, dear, your father . . . your father is dead."

I went cold all over. At first, unable to comprehend fully, I sat silent and bewildered. After a while, shock gave way to overwhelming grief. I began to sob. Grandma gave me the letter and took me up to my room. Eventually I opened it and read:

Dear Jimmy,

You will know now why I did not write to you directly with the terrible news of Dad's death. I am still so shocked myself by the whole disaster that I don't really know how to begin to tell you all that has happened on Oonaderra since your Dad and I returned from seeing you off in Cairns.

When we arrived back home, we found the property as dry and as parched as when we left it, despite the heavy rain that has been falling all along the coast except here on Oonaderra.

But, worse than that, on the morning of our arrival home, Dad went over to the camp and found old Paddy sick and writhing with stomach pains. Dad dosed him with pain killer and gave

124

him medicine for what he thought was diarrhea; but the poor chap died before sundown. And then the sickness spread to others in the camp. Dad radioed Cairns for help, and the authorities sent a naval patrol boat up with two doctors and a detachment of sailors as well as two policemen.

The doctors identified the disease at once as malignant cholera; they said it was evident that the cholera must have been brought to Oonaderra by those Chinese trepang fishermen.

We all had to pitch in to bring the disease under control. But despite the doctors' treatment of the Aborigines, they were unable to help those poor wretches who had had the disease too long for the drugs to save them from dying.

And then, in the midst of all the dreadful tragedy going on, a terrible accident happened to Dad. He and a sailor were over at the saddle shed preparing to load a drum of carbolic acid to take over to the camp to sterilize the area. The drums, as you know, are up on racks. Dad and the sailor were trying to get one down when it slipped and Dad was crushed beneath it. He died instantly. He sleeps now by the side of his father and mother in our cemetery under the coolibah trees over the rise.

All this happened ten days ago, Jimmy. Now the sickness has been cleared up completely. But, as a precaution, the doctors are providing me with a supply of the drugs, just in case they are needed again. I've prayed to God not to let that happen again.

Tomorrow the patrol boat and the men return to Cairns.

Charley told me at the camp this morning that his people will not be going Walkabout; therefore, I must stay here to see that they get their weekly rations. Charley's son—the boy who is your friend—is all right, and has been helping, with his father, to do all he can around the place.

Now, Jimmy dear, try not to worry about my being here alone—I have been on my own many, many times over the years on Oonaderra, so it is nothing new or frightening for me now.

And don't forget, it was always your father's hope that you would one day take over the property, so I must do all I can to see that you do, in due course, become the next Brent on Oonaderra.

Everything now depends on our getting rain to save the stock and enable us to send away, as soon as possible, the bullocks for sale. Later on, all being well, I will arrange to have a married couple come on to Oonaderra to help manage the place.

Well, dear, write soon. When the mailman arrives I will have another letter ready to send off to you.

The captain of the patrol boat is taking this letter with him to post it for me in Cairns. Take care of yourself, dear.

All my love—Mum.

The shock and grief over my father's death was made worse now by my fear for my mother's safety. I knew she was quite capable of managing on her own as she often had had to do in the past on Oonaderra. But the unforeseen things that might happen to her filled me with a dread of the future.

Just before the first school holiday was due in May, I was again called to the headmaster's office to be told that my schooling was to be temporarily interrupted because my mother could no longer afford to keep me at "Churchie." I was to be sent home until financial matters improved on Oonaderra.

126

I cannot say that I was disappointed in having to go home; although I had had a good time at school, I was eager to be back with my mother on Oonaderra.

I met Mum in Cairns. The *Curlew* was moored at the wharves where she had been loaded by the people we bought our supplies from. We sailed for home at once.

How my poor mother had changed over the past few months. Her grief, cares and worries were becoming too much. All through the trip she tried not to show the anxiety she felt for the future. She told me that nearly all our money had been exhausted through death duties and the expenses the authorities had incurred in sending help to combat the cholera.

Yet she never complained to me; nor did she tell me that she had been living on the *Curlew* ever since the patrol boat had left—she waited until we arrived home to tell me that.

We rowed ashore and walked up to the house, with the dog and cat scampering ahead of us. I walked to the front door, opened it, and a wave of hot, stale air from the unlived-in house swept past us.

We went into the living-room with its familiar pink-and-gray-striped sofa and easy chairs. At first I could not make out what the queer silence meant. I said, "Mum, what's the matter with the place? It's so quiet, not a bit like it used to be."

"It's your grandfather's clock, dear. I haven't wound it for the past few months."

"Why?"

"Because I've been living on the boat. You've no idea what it's been like trying to live in this place alone—especially at night, since your father died. But it will be all right now that I have you here with me."

She went to the clock in the corner, wound it, set the time by her wristwatch, and started the pendulum swinging. The clock refused to go. She shook it, jiggled it, and stamped her foot but to no avail—the clock just refused to start.

"Drat it!" she exclaimed finally in exasperation. "Now I've gone and overwound the thing!"

I went through to the back door and opened it. On the veranda was a note with a stone on top of it. I picked the note up. It was from the mailman. It read:

Missus,
Called Monday. Will call in again on my way back on Friday.

Mort Chandler.

Mum came out. She read the note and said, "Today's Monday. Mort must have called this morning."

"Yes. Oh, Mum, what are we going to do about getting the stuff off the boat and across to the storeroom?"

"Oh, we'll leave it till tomorrow. It's too late now to start. Come on in and light the lamp. I'm too short to reach it."

We went back into the living room. I reached up to draw the lamp down on its weighted chain suspended from the ceiling, and a peculiar feeling of fear came over me. That was the first time in my life that I had been given the responsibility of lighting the lamp. My father had always done it.

"Come along!" Mum said. "Whatever's the matter with you?"

I forced myself to overcome the queer feeling that was holding me back, and drew the lamp down and lit it. It was a relief to lift it back above our heads.

"Ah, that's better!" Mum said. "Now let's get ourselves organized. How about lighting the stove for me?"

"Righto."

And so it was that on the first night of my return

to Oonaderra, I became the male head of the house which had claimed the lives of three Brents.

The next morning I was shocked to see how bad the drought was. There was now almost no feed. Poor old Nellie's ribs were sticking through her hide. She nearly took my hand as well as the loaf of bread I gave her to catch her for the job of hauling the supplies to the storeroom.

Mum and I managed to get the supplies from the boat to the dray and safely up to the storeroom by the end of the morning.

When that was done, I checked the house tank—the water was down to a scant six inches! The water in the washhouse tank was down, too. We decided to save that for a reserve supply for the house.

Before she left for Cairns, Mum had instructed Tajalli to supervise the men in felling the light forest growth along the creek banks for the stock. They had become too weak to venture far from the chain of shrinking pools—all that was left of the once-flowing, year-round freshwater creek that was Oonaderra's lifeline.

Nellie now had the home paddock to herself. The rest of the horses were out with the cattle getting what feed they could. In the afternoon I walked over to see the men cutting the forest stuff. The lagoon had become a caked mudhole; along the creek banks the cattle and horses were strung out, nibbling at the leaves and twigs from the green saplings the Oonas were felling.

About a mile farther on, I met the men. In the afternoon heat I was struck by the incongruity of them wearing boots, khaki pants, shirts, and hats. They, of course, being employed on the property, were dressed the way that had always been customary since the Brents settled on Oonaderra.

Instead of getting a cheerful answer to my greeting, the men went on with their chopping in silence. Only Tajalli answered, " 'Lo, Jimmy."

Not a word from Tajurra, who was hacking at a wattle sapling beside his father, keeping his face turned away from me.

I walked over and tapped him on the shoulder. He lowered his axe. "What for you no want talk longa me?" I snapped.

He shuffled uneasily from one foot to the other and looked desperately at Tajalli for help. The others had stopped their chopping to watch.

"All right!" I said, now becoming angry. "Suppose you tell me, Tajalli! What for Oona people no want speak longa me? Me no more pickaninny. By and by me boss longa all you! Better you tell me what wrong, Tajalli!"

Tajalli wearily pushed his hat to the back of his head and said patiently, more patiently than I deserved, "All the Oona men tell Tajurra no more speak longa you; no more he be friend longa you, Jimmy."

"What?" I asked. "What he do wrong? What me do wrong?"

Tajalli answered quietly, "Tajurra tell me long time ago him tell you about spirit belonga Oona people—about thing you see one time longa corroboree. That bad fella thing."

It suddenly dawned on me—he was referring to Tajurra's telling me the meaning of the corroboree which I had watched from the safety of the old tree that night. Only the men of the tribe were supposed to know the meaning of that corroboree. On that night Tajurra had been made a man—but he had broken the tribal decree that no white person must ever learn the secrets of the Aborigines' corroborees.

Their point of view was incomprehensible to me. I said, "All right, Tajalli, maybe you let Tajurra talk longa me, let all the Oona men hear Tajurra speak longa me, speak truth. All right?"

Tajalli looked around at the others.

"All right, Tajalli, we want hear two fella boy talk."

Tajalli nodded to Tajurra and me to speak.

Tajurra began, "Jimmy, me no talk bad about you. Me get big fright when Nimapadi go longa debbil-debbil place longa your house. All the men longa camp talk about Oona make all things die longa Oonaderra now. Me tell Tajalli 'cos I think maybe I do mad thing when I tell you about debbil-debbil Oona put longa house longa your grandfather and grandmother. Me get too big fright altogether. Me think maybe you die, all white people die; me no want you die, Jimmy, no more want mother, father belonga you die. No want anybody die. All the time me have big fright longa here . . ." He touched his hand to his chest and stomach.

Tajalli spoke rapidly to him, and Tajurra, who was about to continue, kept quiet. Tajalli said to me, "All right, Jimmy, you want talk now?"

I nodded and said to Tajurra, "You tell Tajalli I tell nobody about bad thing that Oona longa sky do because house stand longa Bora Ring?"

Tajurra shook his head. "Me no know, Jimmy; maybe you tell people belonga you."

"I tell you, I tell nobody," I answered. "I tell you, me friend longa you, all the same brother longa you, you tell me you all the same brother longa me; remember—we make cut longa arm, we drink blood belonga you, belonga me in shell?"

I pulled up my shirt sleeve and showed the cicatrix he had cut in my upper arm after the night of the corroboree. The sight of the tribal mark on my arm brought an instant gasp of surprise from the assembled men.

Tajalli said to Tajurra, "You make cut longa arm belonga Jimmy, drink blood belonga him, belonga you?"

Tajurra nodded fearfully.

Tajalli spoke rapidly to the others in Oona. Then he tapped Tajurra on the shoulder and said to me, "This silly fella boy, he no tell me about making cut longa you, drinking blood. Suppose him tell me, me no more tell him stop talk longa you. All right now. You and Tajurra all the same brothers. All right now."

Tajurra's face lit up. He and I reached out and grasped hands. "Me glad now, Jimmy," he said. "All the time want be friend longa you."

"All the time, me too," I assured him.

Tajalli said, "Me sorry father belonga you die, Jimmy. What mother belonga you do now?"

"She wait, want rain come quick," I answered.

He said, "Maybe rain no more come longa Oonaderra for long time, Jimmy. Nimapadi die because he make spirit longa that house mad; make rain go away; make other people die; make stock die; by and by make everything die. Oona people think maybe you, maybe mother belonga you die soon, too. No more want you stop longa that house, Jimmy. Better you live longa boat." He spoke anxiously, his eyes showing the genuine dread he had of worse to come in the already long-drawn-out crisis on Oonaderra.

I nodded because I wasn't sure how I should answer. I thanked him for his remembrance of my father and asked him what could be done to avert more trouble. The thought of anything happening to my mother terrified me. The fear of the Curse had begun to take a deep hold over me. There was in his manner, as with the other members of the tribe, a complete acceptance and certainty that Oona, their god, would eventually wreak vengeance on us all.

He answered my question in a roundabout way. "Oona make too many people die too quick longa this place, Jimmy. Grandfather, grandmother belonga you die; grandfather, grandmother belonga Tajurra die; Nimapadi die; Oona people, Oona pickaninny die longa that bad sickness longa here. . . ." He looked round at the gaunt stock following the trail of fallen saplings for the pickings to be had from them, and he went on, "By and by everything longa this place die. House belonga you stay longa place belonga Oona too long. Bora Ring longa Oona, all the same church belonga white people. Better take house away; maybe Oona stop bad spirit longa there; maybe everything all right suppose mother belonga you shift house."

I explained that my mother was in no position to hire labor for such a purpose, even if she could be induced to remove the house, which I was certain she would never do.

I was about to leave them when Tajalli said, "You tell mother what I tell you, Jimmy?"

"Yes, by and by I tell her, Tajalli."

"All right," he said and added, "You want Tajurra walk longa you now?"

I agreed eagerly.

Tajurra slipped off his boots and carried them by the loops on the back; we left the others to their work.

We talked just like old times and made our way across the horse paddock to the Brents' burial ground at the foot of the rise under the coolibah tree. Tajurra slipped his boots on again before venturing into the barbed-wire enclosure around the graves.

"What for you put boot on?" I asked.

He looked surprised and answered. "Oona people no stand longa white fella grave longa bare feet. Tajalli tell me white people make him wear boot longa white people grave."

When Tajalli had been given boots to help dig my father's grave, he had assumed it was the custom of white people not to stand on their burial ground barefooted; and this was precisely the opposite of what Tajurra had once told me when we were at the "burial" of his grandparents. There *he* had told *me* to "take boot off."

We stood in silence by the mound of gray earth over my father's grave beside the weathered, lichen-covered headstones of my grandparents.

When we left the enclosure, Tajurra again slipped off his boots, and we walked to the top of the rise where he asked anxiously, "Jimmy, you no more think Tajalli talk mad fella talk longa you?"

"No; I know he speak truth," I answered.

"Maybe mother belonga you think it mad fella talk, Jimmy. Suppose she tell policeman Tajalli say all people longa Oonaderra, all thing longa this place die?"

I assured him my mother would not be telling the police about the Curse and its origins.

He was immensely relieved and went on to explain, "All the time Oona people have big fella fright longa your mother, they say—suppose bad fella thing get her longa that house, by and by policeman come, take Oona people longa prison . . ." He paused and we both looked across at the house and the wisp of blue smoke rising from the kitchen stovepipe.

Then he went on, "Suppose policeman come, Jimmy, people belonga Tajalli no go longa prison; all the Oona men talk, say drink barata, die all the same Tirkalla, all the same Ninji."

"Tajurra!" I answered angrily, "now *you* talk mad fella talk!"

"No, me tell truth!"

He suddenly looked from me out to sea. He pointed and said excitedly, "Look, Jimmy! Look, Oona!"

Out beyond the reef the head of a huge turtle was cleaving through the water as it came in through the channel. Then it suddenly disappeared.

Tajurra was shaking with excitement. He didn't wait to tell me what the appearance of the turtle meant to him. "Me go now, tell Tajalli Oona come!"

He raced down the rise, past the saddle shed, going like the wind back to the men along the creek bank.

I waited and watched the water in the channel for some time, but the turtle didn't reappear. So I went back to the house.

That evening the Oonas stood on the beach watching the water. They were still standing there at sunset. Then, one by one, their camp fires began to glow orange and red through the trees around the camp.

After we had finished dinner, Mum and I settled down in the living room, she to read and I waiting for an opportunity to speak about the Curse.

Suddenly she looked up from her book and asked, "Whatever's the matter, Jimmy?"

I blurted out, "Oh, Mum, did Dad tell the police about Nimapadi coming to the house drunk when he was given that brandy by the trepangers?"

"No, of course not," she answered. "We wouldn't do a thing like that, Dad always prided himself on being able to manage the blacks without asking help from anybody. You know that."

"Yes, but if I told you something I was told this afternoon would you report it to the police?"

"What on earth are you talking about? How would I know what I should do unless you tell me first what it is?" She put down her book. "Come on, you'd better tell me."

"Not unless you promise first not to tell anyone what I tell you, Mum. Will you promise, please?"

"Oh, all right. I promise."

I recounted the story of the Curse on Oonaderra, and only here and there during my story did my mother interrupt to clarify some point or to check my tale against the background of Oonaderra's history which is all recorded in the book in my father's study. In that book is verified the history of the property which my mother well knew.

At the end of my story she said gently, "Be that as it may, dear, but do you really believe that even worse might happen to us than has already happened?"

"Yes, Mum. Our stock will all die, if we don't get rain soon. We're nearly out of water, too; and what will we do when the tanks are empty? Would you want to use the water that's left in the creek?"

"Now just a moment," she reasoned quietly. "What has happened, and is still happening here on Oonaderra, happened because it is the will of God. For you to say that it is not, is to believe in all this blackfellow nonsense of the Curse being over us. That is blasphemy. You must never forget that we are Christians."

"But," I argued, "aren't we, as Christians, supposed to do to others as we would have them do to us?"

"Jimmy, you're trying to make me appear wrong!"

"But I'm not. We say our god lives up in the sky; the Oonas say the same thing about their god. What's the difference?"

"Never mind what the difference is. We are Christians, and we don't go asking God to curse others when they do wrong things against us."

"But He does, Mum," I insisted.

"How?" she demanded.

"When he says in the Bible, 'I am a jealous God, visiting the sins of the fathers upon the children, even unto the fourth generation.' Isn't that the same thing the Aborigines' god is doing to us because we have this house standing on their sacred ground, as well as all the other wicked things we have done to them?"

"Jimmy! That will be enough!"

Then she rose from her chair and came over to

the sofa and put her arms round me and began to cry. She said, "Let's not talk about it any more."

"All right, Mum," I said. And there the matter rested.

TEN

WITH ONLY enough water left in the tanks to last us for maybe a week at the most—by rationing it for domestic use only—my mother took steps to ensure that we would be able to use the stagnant creek water for the house, if rain did not fall in the meantime.

"I think we had better keep that sack of oatmeal over in the storeroom for old Nellie—we can't expect her to haul water or anything else in the shape she's in now, can we?" she said.

"No, Mum. Do you want me to take some over for her now?"

"Yes; take a bucketful and mind you don't go spilling it."

"I won't."

The oatmeal was our supply for making breakfast porridge, but we didn't mind going without. I took the bucketful over to the saddle shed; before I could pour it into a round tub for her, Nellie was there nudging me out of the way to get at the feed.

In the distance I could hear the Oonas chopping down the green stuff along the creek banks for the rest of the stock. I was dying to find out from Tajurra about the meaning of the big turtle's appearance in the channel the evening before, but I had to wait until late in the afternoon when I took the weekly rations over to the camp on the dray in time for the men's return from work.

I remember how quiet the women and children were when I got there. They had just arrived back at the camp from gathering oysters and other seafood from the shallows around Rocky Point. They said, "Hello," but otherwise they were not their usual friendly selves. Nor were the men inclined to talk much either when they arrived and helped me unload the rations.

I said to Tajalli, "I tell mother belonga me all about bad fella debbil-debbil stay longa house, Tajalli."

He nodded and said quietly, "She think you tell truth, Jimmy?"

"Don't know, she get little bit mad longa me."

He nodded again and waited for me to go on, so I said, "Tajalli, what for all the Oona people watch that big fella turtle last night? You think that fella turtle made good fella thing come longa this place?"

Instead of giving me a direct answer, he said, "Maybe, maybe no; by and by Oona men make fire longa corroboree place. . . ." He pointed up to the corroboree ground at the bend of the creek and went on, "Maybe debbil-debbil longa corroboree fire tell Oona men what for that big fella turtle come longa here." Then he shrugged, looked at the men standing around the dray, spread his hands, palms upward, in front of him in a gesture to end his statement with, "Maybe we find out, maybe no."

Without another word he and the others began sharing out the rations.

Tajurra had been standing beside Tajalli, and I said to him, "How 'bout you come longa me have ride, eh?"

He asked Tajalli, who nodded his agreement.

Tajurra climbed up, and we drove over to the saddle shed and let Nellie go. We stood there talking about the turtle's appearance, and what it might mean to his people.

After a while I asked him if Tajalli had meant they were going to have a full-scale corroboree.

He answered, "No have big fella corroboree, Jimmy. Oona men make fire, sit longa it. Maybe Tajalli take bag, make all the things longa bag fall longa ground; maybe stones, little fella pickaninny turtle tell him what for that big fella turtle come longa Oonaderra."

"You go longa fire, longa men?" I asked.

"No, Jimmy—all old men go—boy no more go longa fire this time."

"All right then; you find out what that fella thing longa bag tell him, you tell me, eh?"

"No!" His reaction was immediate. "Me no more talk longa you about this fella corroboree."

That night I saw the fire blazing on the corroboree ground and the squatting figures of Tajalli and the old men, their bodies ceremoniously white-painted, sitting silhouetted in the red glow of the flames. They were, I imagined, discussing their future from the way the contents of Tajalli's bag of assorted teji stones, "cat's-eyes," bandicoot's skull, dried lizards, and the mummified baby turtle fell upon the ground . . . they were still sitting there when I went to bed. . . .

Over the next couple of days, nothing eventful happened on Oonaderra. In the evenings my mother and I rowed out to the *Curlew* to tune in for the weather reports. They merely confirmed what we already knew from watching the cloudless sky: ". . .

Light, variable winds, seas smooth, the weather is expected to remain fine over the next few days. . . ."

On Friday morning, while we were having breakfast in the kitchen, Mort Chandler arrived. He called out, "Anybody home?" and came striding into the kitchen.

"Hello, Missus. Hello, Jimmy."

"Oh, hello, Mort," we answered. We were always glad of his company and all the news he brought from the world beyond Oonaderra.

"Any mail for us, Mort?" Mum asked.

"Only a couple of circulars, I think." He handed her the letters.

"Got time for a cuppa, Mort?" she asked.

"Sure, thanks, Missus. I've got time for a breather—I'm two hours ahead of time for once."

He sat between us, and over the tea and toast filled us in on the news on Cape York Peninsula. Later he remarked, "You're sure having a tough trot, Missus—I've never seen Oonaderra even half as bad as it is now—if you don't get rain in the next two or three weeks, this place will have had it. If it wasn't for that green stuff the blacks are felling, that stock of yours would all be dead. How are you managing for water?"

"Not so good, Mort, we've got maybe enough in the tanks to last us for a few more days, that's all."

"I wish there was something I could do to help," he said. "I can't for the life of me understand why Jack never got round to looking for underground water—there must be artesian water on the property; you never know but what you could have it right under your feet."

"Oh, Jack was always going to get around to doing it, but he never did, Mort, because we could always depend on the rain in the past."

"Well, it's the future you've got to think about now," he said. "I always believe in first things first.

What you need right now is to find out if there is any underground water around here. Look, I can spare an hour—how about I do a spot of water-divining for you, eh? It won't hurt to give it a go round the house. OK?"

Mum thanked him but asked dubiously, "How are we to get at the water if you do find any, Mort?"

"We'll cross that bridge when we come to it, Missus," he answered crisply. "Come on, Jimmy, give us a hand to get a forked stick from one of those she-oaks growing down along the beach."

"You bet I will!"

From one of his saddlepacks he took his tomahawk. I followed him down the slope to where the she-oaks grew above the high-water mark. He cut himself a forked stick about eight inches long and gave me the tomahawk to carry while he grasped the two ends of the V of the stick, one in each hand, knuckles upward, with the prong of the stick held ahead of him while he walked back to the house where Mum joined us.

We followed Mort as he slowly circled around the house in ever widening circles but nothing happened; the prong of the stick remained stationary.

After a fruitless search had taken us almost across to the washhouse at the foot of the rise, he gave up. Wiping his brow, he said hopelessly, "Well, you can't say we haven't tried—there's no damn water under this ground, because, if there were, then I would have located it—even if it was a hundred feet down!"

We nodded dejectedly, and Mum said, "Ah, well, Mort, if there's no water under this ground, then there isn't and you can't be blamed for trying. We're very grateful for what you've done as it is. If God had meant us to have artesian water, he would surely have shown us where to find it. Come on, we don't want to waste any more of your time, Mort."

"Let's give it one more go." He set off again with the stick held before him. We followed, walking about thirty feet from the foot of the rise and heading in the direction of the Oonas' camp. After we had traveled about fifty paces, Mort turned into the foot of the rise to travel along it back toward the washhouse. The moment he reached the foot of the rise the prong of the stick suddenly began to bend downward. Mort said excitedly, "Hey! Look at this, will you!"

With Mum on one side of him and me on the other, we watched in amazement as the point of the stick tried to twist the two ends of the fork out of his grasp.

"Gawd almighty!" he gasped. "There's a bloody river flowing under here or my name's not Mort Chandler!"

About twenty paces from the washhouse, he could no longer hold on to the stick. The downward pull of the prong was actually twisting the bark away from the ends he was grasping. He dropped the stick and said, "There you are, Missus—if you don't find water eight or ten feet right under here where I'm standing, then I'll never do another job of water-divining, so help me God I won't!"

Mum, of course, was amazed, and so was I. All she could say was, "I can't believe it, Mort—it's uncanny; to think that now, when we so desperately need water, you have been sent to find it for us. I can't believe it!"

"You don't have to," he said with a wry grin. "Just get a couple of those blacks of yours on to a bar and shovel, and you'll soon see whether you can believe it or not. If I'm not mistaken, and I know I'm not, you've got permanent water now because it's running too strong to be otherwise."

While they talked, I picked up the forked stick and tried it—there was a very feeble down-pointing of the prong but no more than that.

Back at the house Mum made a pot of tea and sandwiches for us before Mort left. She seemed terribly shaken by the turn of events. While we were eating, she suddenly asked to be excused and went to her room. She was crying.

She came back a few minutes later. I thought Mort had not noticed anything until he asked quietly, "You got something else worrying you, Missus?"

She hedged a bit and kept looking at me in a self-conscious way before she answered, "Well, yes, Mort, I have; but I don't want you to get the idea that I'm not grateful for what you've done for us because I am."

"Oh, you don't have to be thanking me, Missus," he replied. "I'm only too glad I've been able to help you out. Sorry I can't stay to give you a hand to get the well sunk. It's a pity we weren't able to locate the water closer to the house for you; it'll mean you'll have to haul it all the way across to the house."

Before he could say any more, she said, "That's what I've been thinking, Mort—among other things."

"Such as?"

She tried hard not to look at me. "Well, Jimmy and I were discussing this house the other night, and he thought we should move it to a better location. I wasn't keen on the idea; but now that we seem to have a permanent water supply I thought it might not be such a bad idea after all if we were to shift the house closer to where the well will be sunk. Mind you, shifting the house would have to wait until we get rain and can fatten up the stock to get a mob of the bullocks out for sale. What do you think it would cost to get a couple of men, Mort, to come up later to do the job?"

Mort scratched his head, looked at me, then at her, and said jokingly, "You must be kidding, Missus; I'll admit it would be a good idea to have the house nearer to the well when you get it sunk, but shift it lock, stock, and barrel! It'll cost you more than you think, to get carpenters all the way up here to do a job like that!"

144

"I know that, Mort. But no matter what, as soon as we get rain I'm going to Cairns to arrange an overdraft to do it."

"Well, good luck to you," he replied. "I hope you get your wish and the rain comes soon. Is there anything else I can do to help out before I go?"

"Yes, there is—could you find out for me how much it would cost us to get the job done later on?"

"Sure I will," he said and rose to go. "I'll let you know the next time I call."

"Thanks, Mort."

We walked out to the back veranda steps with him. He swung into the saddle, gathered up the lead rope of his packhorses, and called out, "Take care of yourselves! Good luck! Hooray, Missus! Hooray, Jim!"

"Hooray, Mort!" we called after him as he jogged along to the rise and up to the top with the hot dry wind swirling the dust and leaves up behind him in a "whirly whirly."

At the top he waved, then disappeared down the other side.

Now that Mort had gone, I could voice my excitement over my mother's decision to have the house shifted eventually. "Oh, Mum, you beauty!" I burst out. "So you really mean you want to shift the house for the sake of Tajalli's people. Do you, Mum?"

"Now, Jimmy," she admonished me, "I did not say that I was doing it for the sake of the Oonas."

"Well, why are you going to do it?" I insisted.

"Because, when I left you two in the kitchen, I went to my room and thanked God for leading us to water, and I promised Him that I would try to atone for any wrong we may have done the blacks. If God has seen fit to reward us with water, the least we can do is to give the blacks back their sacred ground."

"Gee, thanks, Mum! Can I go and tell Tajurra and the others all about it?"

"No; not until you've fed Nellie, and then you

can. go and tell old Charley we want to get started right away on sinking the well."

"Righto, Mum!" I went off like a shot to get the bucket of oatmeal and was over the rise before she could find something else for me to do.

I tossed the feed into the tub for Nellie and raced across to the cattle yards and beyond, until I reached the men chopping away at the saplings along the creek bank.

Breathless and almost incoherent from excitement, I gasped out. "Tajalli! Tajurra! Everybody! Mother belonga me say she shift house belonga us!"

They all stopped and gasped their disbelief. I walked up to Tajalli and Tajurra and repeated that my mother had said she was going to have the house moved away from their sacred Bora Ring.

Tajalli asked cautiously, "What for she do it now, Jimmy?"

I told him and the others about the mailman finding the underground stream at the foot of the rise and said that was the reason Mum had decided on the move. But I added, "She no do it now—maybe by and by when rain come, make grass grow, sell bullocks, get money."

All Tajalli would say was, "What she want me do?"

I told him my mother wanted to get started on sinking a well down to the water right away.

"All right," he agreed. "Tajurra come longa me, help dig hole, find water."

He instructed the others to carry on with their work. I was all for Tajurra and myself racing ahead to get the shovel and crowbar on to the site right away, but Tajalli said something to Tajurra, and he said to me, "Better me stay longa Tajalli, Jimmy; him get fright—think maybe I walk longa bad fella ground."

I was disappointed, but I knew that the Curse's invisible line of demarcation still existed and the

Oonas would refuse to cross it no matter what the reason.

The well site was just outside the forbidden area.

I set off alone to get the bar and shovel ready.

My mother was waiting at the site when I lugged the gear over the rise. I remember her standing there in her blue gingham dress and wide straw hat. She looked so alone. When I reached her and put down the bar and shovel, she said, "Oh, I thought old Charley wasn't coming. Here he is now and that boy of his."

Tajalli and Tajurra came down and greeted her, " 'Lo, Missus."

" 'Lo, Charley, 'Lo, Titch," she answered and explained what she wanted done.

Tajalli waited respectfully for her to finish. Then he asked her was it true she was going to move the house. She told him what I had already told him. Again he listened carefully to her words before he said, "Big fella turtle come longa this place longa water, Missus. Oona men talk longa other big fella Oona longa sky. We ask Oona make bad debbil-debbil go back longa sky, make good thing come, make rain come. Maybe him show it you water longa ground."

I was struck by Tajalli's simple dignity and humility as he spoke of the plea he and the elders had made to their god to relieve the agony on drought-stricken Oonaderra.

My mother was also moved by his simple sincerity. She said with a gentle little smile, "Maybe god belonga you all the same god belonga me, eh, Charley?"

"Think maybe him all the same one fella god belonga everybody, Missus," Tajalli said with a wide smile.

"I suppose so," she replied. "Well, now, I leave you dig well, Charley. By and by I bring you tucker longa washhouse."

"All right, Missus."

She walked back to the house, and we started sinking the well under the guidance of Tajalli, who took the crowbar and loosened the first few inches of earth in a three-foot-diameter circle. When I tried to grab the shovel away from Tajurra in my eagerness to get down to where we hoped the water would lie, he yelled, "No, me dig first!"

Tajalli grinned and said, "By and by you no want work; suppose you let him Tajurra show him got big fella muscle."

"Me show you!" Tajurra said, so I let him have the shovel for the first go.

Shrewd old Tajalli handed me the bar to loosen the earth for the shoveler. Highly amused, he lit his pipe and waited for our enthusiasm to wear off.

It was fairly simple going down into the first few inches of topsoil and on through the next layer or so of subsoil to the stiff clay beneath it. It was then that we were glad of Tajalli's help in digging down through that.

By lunchtime we were down about three feet when the clay ended and the bar struck rock! It was solid brown shale . . . and we had five or more feet to go, according to Mort's reckoning, before we would strike water.

Tajurra and I were already exhausted. The sight of my mother carrying a billy of tea and sandwiches across to the washhouse was most welcome for all of us.

What a relief it was just to sit on the washhouse floor with a sandwich in one hand and a pannikin of tea in the other and forget the backbreaking work.

Mum asked Tajalli how we were making out.

"All right, Missus," he said. "But maybe take another three, four day, maybe more. Got rock longa there now."

"Oh," she answered with evident disappointment. "You think water down there, Charley?"

"Don't know, Missus, maybe."

"Ah, well," she said resignedly, "I hope you find water. Tank longa house altogether finish now."

She went to the washhouse tank and tapped the rings down to the last two which responded with the dull sound of water still behind them—five inches of water left between us and days of digging through flint-hard shale for a stream which nobody knew with any certainty, except Mort Chandler, would be there at the eight- or ten-foot depth he had mentioned.

Mum asked Tajalli if we could make do with the remains of the tea in the billy for the afternoon. In the morning we could fill up a waterbag to help see us through the day. He assured her we would manage all right.

Tajurra and I decided it would be a good idea to go down for a swim while the tide was in.

"All right we go, Tajalli?" he asked.

"All right, come back soon longa work. You go that way." He pointed to the top of the rise. He was taking no chances on Tajurra crossing the line of demarcation in his enthusiasm to get to the beach.

Away we went up and then down along the top of the rise to the "safe area" beyond the two-hundred-yard "line" and across to the beach. We stripped under the she-oak where we had pledged our brotherhood little more than a year before, and on we went down into the booming white breakers curling over the blue water.

After half an hour or so of diving and swimming, we went back to the tree where we sat, letting the hot wind dry us.

Suddenly Tajurra said, "Suppose by and by mother belonga you shift house—she let me come there sit longa chair longa you, eat tucker, Jimmy?"

"What! Oh, too right, she no think like father belonga me, she want you come longa house all the time," I answered, surprised by his wanting to come and eat with us.

He said seriously, "Suppose I come longa house longa new place, I wear trouser, wear shirt, wear boot, Jimmy; no more look like myall fella."

I laughed. His reference to "myall fella" meant simply, a wild, uncivilized black. I said, "Mother belonga me no care about black fella how he look; all the same have pants, all the same have no pants."

He roared with laughter and said, between his paroxysms of merriment, "Better me keep pants on, eh, Jimmy?

How long we talked and laughed I don't know, but suddenly the clang of the old cowbell jerked us back to reality. We looked up. My mother was on the front veranda, ringing the bell with one hand and pointing with the other to Tajalli laboriously wielding the bar on the rock down the shaft of the well.

We scrambled into our clothes and hurried along the rise to work where we should have been long before.

ELEVEN

ALL THROUGH that afternoon till sundown, we gouged and splintered away the dry, unyielding shale to increase the depth by no more than fifteen inches or so. The next day and the two following got us down to about six feet. Tajalli had taken over the job of working down the shaft, leaving Tajurra and me to hoist up on a rope the buckets of shale which we spread around the surface. All the while my mother anxiously waited for sight of the water.

On the fifth day, late in the afternoon, Tajalli came up and out of the shaft for a break. He went over to the sapling where our waterbag hung beside the lunchtime billy of tea we had to keep us going; he was about to take a swig from the bag when he stopped, replaced the bag, and walked up to the top of the rise. He was watching intently the sky to the south.

He stood there for a few minutes, just staring;

then he came back to us and said, "White men come longa everywhere longa this place."

"How you know that?" I asked.

"Men belonga another tribe send smoke talk longa sky; say white men ride quick all about everywhere, come longa Oonaderra, maybe tomorrow."

Tajurra looked scared and asked, "That white fella policemen, Tajalli?"

"No policemen," Tajalli answered. "Plenty men ride horse; come quick longa this place; no more policemen."

I said, "What for all the men come longa here, Tajalli?"

He shrugged. "Don't know; man longa other tribe no know—just say white men ride horse altogether too quick longa this place. Better we get well finish, clear out; no more want trouble longa white men."

He quickly lowered himself down the shaft to get on with the work while the light remained. I ran across to the house and told Mum.

She and I went out to look at the cloudless sky. We could see nothing even remotely resembling smoke.

"Oh, Jimmy, Charley must be mistaken; he must have imagined it all."

"No," I answered. "He didn't. He knows how to read smoke signals from the other tribes on the Peninsula. He knew, and so did all the other people at the camp, when that policeman was coming to arrest old Tirkalla—his father, you remember?"

"Yes; but he knew that the police would come, Jimmy, for sure, because that old man had escaped from Palm Island."

"No, Mum," I argued. "He saw the smoke signals the day before the policeman got here. I know—I was over at the camp when it happened and all the Oona people went bush long before the policeman got here. It's true, Mum—he said there are white men on the way here, and I know he means it."

"Oh, all right, we'll see."

"Jimmy! Jimmy! Missus!"

We looked across at Tajurra frantically waving and yelling for us to hurry over.

By the time we reached the well, Tajalli had hoisted himself up out of the shaft, and he and Tajurra were staring down into it.

"You find water, Charley?" Mum panted.

He nodded. We all peered down to the bottom of the shaft. A tiny spray of water was squirting up through the shale.

Tajalli lay flat on his stomach, reached down for the bar, lifted it, and tied the rope from the bucket to it. Then he stood up and holding the end of the rope, let the bar fall down the shaft. The shale at the bottom caved in under the impact, and water flooded in and halfway up the shaft.

The four of us stood there gaping at the yellow, debris-stained water spinning like a whirlpool under the pressure of the fast-flowing stream beneath.

"Thank God!" my mother said fervently. Then she began to cry as she said. "And thank you, too, Charley; you've done a wonderful job, and so have you two boys."

In the few moments in which we had turned to look at my mother, the underground stream had drawn down the yellow-stained water leaving it shining and clear.

Tajalli hauled up the bar and said to Tajurra, "Get pannikin."

Tajurra dashed over to the washhouse and brought back the pannikin. Tajalli again flattened himself at the well's edge and scooped up a mug of the water. He stood up with it and said, "You like drink, Missus?"

"Thanks, Charley." She sipped at it first and then drank the lot. "It's beautiful, cold fresh water!"

We all tried it; it was, indeed, clear, cold spring water. Providence had stepped in to save us, at almost the last moment, from having to use the stagnant creek water or abandon the property.

Mum said, "Charley, true you see smoke longa sky, tell you white men come longa Oonaderra?"

"That true, Missus," he answered.

"You know what him come for, eh?"

"No, Missus. Me hope no more trouble come longa you, longa Oona people; Oona people no want any more trouble longa this place."

"You no worry, Charley," she assured him. "You no do wrong thing. By and by I tell everybody all about people belonga you altogether good fella longa me, longa Jimmy."

He quietly nodded his thanks, but it was plain that he and Tajurra were still unhappy about so many white men heading for Oonaderra.

While Tajalli and Tajurra covered the well with saplings, I went with Mum to the house to get a present for them. I brought it back—a tin full of toffees and licorice all-sorts, as well as an extra ration of trade tobacco for Tajalli. Money, of course, was useless to them, but lollies and an extra ration of tobacco were something else altogether.

That eventful day ended with gratitude and hope, and my mother's prayers that God, or Providence, or whatever, would send the rain to complete our salvation.

Tajalli's interpretation of the smoke signals was confirmed the next day when, directly after I had returned to the house from feeding Nellie, the first of the men came over the rise riding at a canter and leading two sweating, panting packhorses—it was Carl Muller!

"Hi, there!" he called out to us on the back veranda.

"Oh, hello, Carl!" we greeted him as he dismounted and hitched his horses to the veranda rail.

"What on earth brings you here?" Mum asked incredulously.

"Stone the crows, Missus!" he answered as he came up on to the veranda. "Don't you know?"

He shoved his hat to the back of his head and said, "Cripes, Missus, the whole Peninsula knows it! —Mort Chandler spread the word around that you were wanting a well dug and this here house of yours moved near to it. Isn't that true?"

"Why, yes, it is. But Mort only left here last Friday. How could you have found out and got here so quickly?"

"That was easy," Carl explained. "It appears that when Mort left here, he called first at Bluey Perkins' place—that's about a day's ride from here. He gave Bluey the message to send over his two-way radio, which he did. I got it over my wireless in Mount Molloy on the local evening news, so I set off for here at first light last Saturday; and I can tell you, I've been pushing those horses of mine like the bloody devil himself to get here. I had no idea you were having a drought until I rode over the property on the way in. You sure need rain soon, Missus, or you'll lose your stock for sure."

"Yes, Carl, but we've had one stroke of good luck —we've got the well sunk—and we struck splendid water, yesterday."

"Good for you!" he exclaimed enthusiastically. "That makes one less worry for you." To me he said, "And how've you been doing, Jimmy?"

"Oh, not bad, Carl. I helped to dig the well and find the water."

"That's the stuff, son—you help your Ma all you can. How come you're home? You finished school for good?"

I told him that I would be returning to school later when things improved. We had missed tuning in on the radio for the past few days because we had been too tired from the well-sinking to bother going to the boat, and so we had missed out on the news that the whole Peninsula had heard about our plight on Oonaderra.

After a cup of tea with us, Carl lost no time in unloading the bedding and provisions he had brought, as well as the feed for his horses, which he let go in the home paddock.

He then set to work checking the house, carefully noting down on paper all the essential measurements for its removal to the site my mother had chosen; the new location was on the level ground between the well and the washhouse.

The house was on low stumps—about two feet high. Carl and I crawled underneath on our stomachs, into the dust and debris of over half a century, and with a surveyor's tape measure, we measured the distances between the stumps. From there, we went over to the new site and drove into the ground wooden pegs to indicate the new positions for the digging of the stump holes.

At about four in the afternoon he had noted all the details he wanted. Soon afterward, Mr. Renfrew, from one of the outlying stations, arrived with half a dozen men from other properties. By nightfall, seven more men rode in, making a total of fifteen: men of the Australian outback, noted for their big-heartedness when it comes to lending a hand to anyone in adversity. All had brought their own supplies on packhorses. Carl took charge of the project—and a better man for the job would have been hard to find.

That night the place looked like a military encampment with the men sleeping on the ground in a long line in front of the washhouse, their loaded saddle packs dumped alongside in readiness for my mother when she took over the cooking arrangements the next day.

At daybreak the men were up. Carl immediately

had our big stove carried from the kitchen and set up in the washhouse. Everything else Mum needed from the kitchen was carted over for her. I was detailed to be her offsider and wood-and-water Joey, as well as looking after the feeding of the horses in the home paddock. But I still found time to slip over now and then to watch what was going on at the house.

Before breakfast, the men had cleared the house of all its furniture which they piled away from the site and covered with tarpaulins from the saddle shed.

Everybody ate on the ground, and straight after breakfast the real work began.

Grandfather Brent had built his house section by section out of red cedar—light, strong, and easily worked timber. And as he added each new section, he had bolted it firmly to the last to make a strong, rigid construction throughout, well able to withstand the fiercest cyclone. The quality and strength of his work was soon proved when the men began moving the house.

While four of the men started sinking the stump holes on the new site, two others harnessed Nellie to the dray and drove to the back of the camp to get poles and a load of wood billets. Carl and the rest of the men set about uncoupling and removing the rainwater tank and stand, before they started unbolting the verandas for their removal away from the house proper. Mum's lemon and orange trees had to be chopped down, but she salvaged her treasured Dorothy Perkins rose for replanting at the new site.

It was midday when the dray returned loaded with square, split hardwood billets and three eight-yard-long bloodwood poles. Nellie was unharnessed and taken back to the home paddock where she could get extra feed from the other horses' rations.

After lunch I watched the men lifting the verandas out of the way. They eased the back veranda away from the house until they had room to slip the poles under it. Then four men, one to each end of a pole at either end of the veranda and the other two with the third pole in the center, lifted the whole structure bodily out of the way. They used the same method to move the side and front verandas, leaving the house itself sitting on its stumps like a huge box.

I had been dying to find out what the poles and billets were for. Now I knew. But there was a further use for them. The men, under Carl's direction, built three tiers of the billets, one tier at each end of the back of the house and the third at its center. With three men to each pole, the pole ends were inserted under the first joist of the house, which supported the floor. Approximately a yard from the joist, the poles rested on the tiers, and the overhang was used as a lever, which the men could just reach up and get hold of. They waited for Carl, who was at the left-corner stump supporting the house, and Mr. Renfrew at the right-corner stump. Each had half a dozen of the wooden billets lying nearby. Carl gave the order to the men on the poles, "OK, boys, when you're ready—right! Pull!"

In unison, the men pulled down on the ends of the poles; it made the operation look so ridiculously easy. The back of the house lifted a good six inches. "Right!" Carl called out. "Hold it!" He and Mr. Renfrew slipped a billet each on their respective corner stumps and the men, on Carl's order, lowered the back of the house gently onto the supporting billets on the corner stumps.

The same simple procedure was carried out at the front of the house. And so, by alternately levering and raising, billet by billet, the back and front of the house, Carl got it up to the height he wanted.

I had to leave to get back to my own work. In the late afternoon the Oona women came along the top of the rise to get water from the well—a change from the stale stuff they had been using from the pools left in the creek.

They came hurrying, carrying empty tins, drums, billies, coolamons, or whatever they could find that would hold water. I drew the water for them. They were shy in the presence of so many white men on the property. The men digging the new stump holes greeted them with, "Hiya, Mary," or "Hiya, Biddy," but the women would only answer, " 'Lo, Boss," get their water and hurry away back along the top of the rise to the camp.

When the women had their water, Carl yelled across to me from where he was standing by the dray, "Hey! Jimmy! You got a pump for these tires?"

"Yes. I'll get it for you!"

I went over to the saddle shed and fetched the double-action foot pump for him.

He and the men took turns at the job of pumping up the tires until they held their maximum pressure.

Two tiers of the billets had been built at the back of the house, one tier at each end, leaving the way clear for the dray to be backed in under the house between the two center rows of stumps. This the men proceeded to do, edging the dray backward in under the joists until only the shafts were sticking out. There was barely an inch clearance between the joists and the top of the dray.

Of course, I couldn't resist finding out at once from Carl how the house would be lowered onto the dray.

Carl winked at the others and said, in mock seriousness, "Well, Jim, it's like this, you see: we need a strapping young bloke, like you, to lift the house while we knock out the billets on the corner stumps. Think you can do it?"

"Aw, break it up!" I answered, self-consciously looking around at the grinning faces of the men and back to Carl. "Do you think I came down in the last shower or something?"

"OK, OK!" Carl laughed. "I should've known better than to try to take a rise out of a Brent—especially a carroty-topped one."

He then explained that the method for lowering the house onto the dray was no more than a reversal of the procedure by which they had raised it.

And in the morning I watched while the men on the poles—this time only two poles were being used on the two tiers at each end of the house—positioned them for the lift while Carl and Mr. Renfrew took their places at the corner stumps.

Carl said, "Now take it easy, boys. We want her to lift just clear of the billets. OK, up and hold her."

The men pulled down slowly on their poles, the house lifted clear of the supporting billets on the corner stumps. I watched their faces, tensed and strained, while they held the house up as Carl and Mr. Renfrew pulled away the billets. "Right, boys!" Carl sang out. "Now lower away dead slow!"

The men eased the poles, and the back of the house came down slowly onto the dray. There was a sharp intake of breaths as the men dropped their poles with relief at the safe completion of the first stage of the project. But the next most dangerous stage, the lowering of the front of the house, had to be carried out before there could be any hope that the project might be successfully concluded.

Even the usually jovial Carl became anxious about the outcome. The billets were taken round to the front of the house, but this time, Carl and the men erected three tiers of them. This was necessary because of the greater weight the men would have to lift, which was caused by the long overhang of the house over the back of the dray.

Then, with the men ready at the poles, Carl gave the order to lift and hold. For what seemed like an eternity, the front of the house was held clear of the

160

stump billets while Carl and Mr. Renfrew knocked them away. Carl gave the order to "Lower her down, boys! Now, easy! . . . Easy!"

Little by little the house settled on to the back of the dray, but the great weight of the overhang, despite the wide treads of the ballon tires, forced the rear wheels of the dray down into the deep dust under the house, leaving the house tilted backward.

The men removed their poles. One of them said, "Think she'll make it, Carl?"

"She'll just bloody well have to!" Carl answered. "She'll straighten up once we get her on to firm ground . . . I hope. Anyway, come on, let's have a look at how the others are making out with the stump holes."

I followed them over to the new site. The stump holes were ready, and the men were working on the excavation of a runway leading between the two center rows of holes. They were digging down to the hard shale, and the excavation was being pushed out beyond the stumps to make an incline for the dray to negotiate to get the house positioned above them when they were put in.

Carl said to the men, "How long do you reckon it'll take you to finish?"

"Oh, before sundown, we think."

"OK; then we'll start bringing the stumps over and get them in."

The stumps—solid black bean—were in as good a condition as the day they were put there by my grand-parents. It was a tough job getting them out and carry-ing them over to the new site for resetting. But by the end of the day they were all in their new positions and the runway was completed. Everything was ready for the next day.

Except for the women collecting their water in the evenings, none of the Oonas had ventured anywhere near the new site for the house, not even Tajurra. They were, of course, continuing their daily felling along the creek banks.

The next morning, however, when the task of moving the house was beginning, Tajalli and three of the elder tribesmen (they were probably the ones who had been with him around the corroboree fire) came along the top of the rise to watch. They just stood there staring across at the house and at us.

Nellie had been harnessed up to the dray. All the men, and my mother and I, were there to lend a hand.

Carl took Nellie by the bridle, while the rest of us went round the back to lift the overhang and push when he gave the order.

"You all ready there?" he called out.

"Yes! As soon as you are!"

"OK, then . . . lift and push like bloody hell!"

We heaved and lifted with all our might. Suddenly the house began to move. We kept it moving until we got it on to solid ground. We had made it! The house was safe—so far!

Tajalli and the others had gone from the top of the rise.

It took most of the morning before we could maneuver the dray and the house into the straight-ahead position leading to the excavated incline down through the two center rows of the house stumps. And the journey across to the site took most of the afternoon as we all pushed to help Nellie draw the load in short runs and stops up to the incline. There Carl stopped us. The front wheels of the dray were just over the runway. He wound on the dray's old-fashioned winder brake. Nellie was taken out of the shafts and sent back to the home paddock.

Now Carl was faced with the risky task of easing the dray and the house down and over the rows of stumps.

Two of the men took one shaft each to guide the

162

dray. Carl stepped between the shafts to work the brake, while we at the back waited for him to shout, "Get her started!"

We pushed, and the load began to roll down the runway bit by bit as Carl applied the brake to let the men on the shafts keep the dray in the dead-ahead position between the center stumps.

At the foot of the runway the excavation leveled out so there was no need for the brake. We pushed and heaved and finally our main task was almost accomplished. Under Carl's superb guidance, the house was now positioned directly over the stumps. Carl wound the brake on to hold the dray for the final job of lowering the house onto the stumps. Then he and three of the others crawled under the house to the sides of the dray, each of them to a wheel. Carl sang out, "Right!"

There was a loud hiss as they let the air out of the tires and down the house settled, square onto its stumps!

"Hooray! You beauty! You little bobby dazzler!" we all yelled, and the men threw their hats into the air with jubilation at a job well done.

Carl was carried shoulder-high around the house to mark the occasion and his superb bossmanship.

Then the dray was pulled from under the house and the tires pumped up in readiness for the fourth and final day's work of carting the verandas and the rest of the stuff over.

Round about four o'clock the next afternoon, the men were working flat out to complete the job before sundown. The verandas and the front and back steps were all back in position. Only the empty house tank had to be hoisted up onto its stand and the pipe recoupled to the kitchen tap. The runway had been filled in, and some of the men were already carrying in the furniture. Even the poles and wood billets had been carted over from the old site to serve as an extra supply of firewood for the house.

I was in the washhouse helping Mum prepare the food for the housewarming party to be held that night as a send-off for the men who were leaving for home early in the morning.

Tajurra came up the rise and beckoned to me. I went up. He was trembling with suppressed excitement.

"When all the men go home, Jimmy?" he asked.

I told him, and asked what he was so excited about.

"Tajalli want know," he answered. "He want go longa there." He pointed over to the old housesite and went on, "When all white men go home, he bring other men longa him, fix that fella place up. He want shovel. You give me two fella shovel, Jimmy?"

"All right. You want come, have look longa house?"

He shook his head. "By and by, Jimmy. Tajalli tell me no go longa house; tell everybody."

It suddenly struck me that none of the Oonas had been near the place since the house had been moved the previous afternoon—not even the women to get water from the well.

"All right," I said. "I get shovel."

I brought the shovels the men had finished using and handed them to him. He took them and said, "Tajalli tell me, tell you, better you no come longa other place when Oona men go there." He again pointed across to the old site.

"What for?" I asked.

"Don't know, Jimmy. Tajalli no want white people go longa there when Oona men dig ground. Tajalli say by and by him show you that fella place."

I said, "Oona men no more fright longa that bad fella debbil-debbil longa that place now, eh, Tajurra?"

"Maybe little bit fright," he answered. "Oona people no more want walk longa that place; Oona men want Tajalli make altogether good fella place; want him walk longa that place longa other men first."

164

And that was all he would, or dare, tell me about the purpose of the leader and elders of the tribe being the first to cross the line of demarcation after more than half a century of the Curse of Oona being on it.

I had little time to ponder though, because I was called to help get the still hot stove out of the wash-house and into the kitchen.

TWELVE

THE HOUSE WARMING was a most happy affair. The house rang with the laughter and jokes of the men as they sat around the dining-room table eating the feast Mum had prepared. And there was wine from the reserve stock we always keep in the storeroom for the rare times when we have visitors on the property.

And there were after-dinner speeches, too. Carl was sitting at one end of the table, Mum, with me beside her, at the other. Carl rose and addressed my mother. "Well, Missus, you're not out of the woods yet; you've still got to have rain soon to get the grass growing in time to save your stock. I'm not a praying man, Missus, but I hope to God you do get it in time. Well, anyway, good rain and good grass will solve your main problem—that's for sure; but after that, there'll be mustering and dipping and a hell of a lot of other things to do before you can get a mob of bullocks ready for sale. So, get on to that radio of yours whenever you need help again, and I, for one, will be back here like a shot to lend a hand."

He sat down amidst a chorus of "Hear, hear! That goes for us, too, Missus!"

Mum rose, thanked them, and said, "Both Jimmy and I are deeply grateful for what has already been done for us in moving this house to where Mort so providentially found water. Carl says he is not a praying man; he doesn't have to be, nor do any of us, because I believe we are all measured not by the prayers we offer God but by our deeds toward one another here on earth. I thank God and ask His blessing on all of you for what you have done for us. Thank you."

At first light in the morning, after an early breakfast, Mum and I walked to the top of the rise to watch the men saddling up their horses, and to wave them good-bye as they rode off and became lost from view in the timber.

Then we turned and saw the men from the camp heading up the creek to start another day's work of felling green feed for the stock. The women and children were making toward the beach for the daily gathering of seafood.

On the previous evening I had told Mum what Tajurra had told me about Tajalli and the tribal elders going on to the old house site to perform whatever was necessary on their sacred Bora Ring ground to exorcize the Curse of Oona.

She said to me, "I think you had better get over to the storeroom, Jim, and get Nellie's oatmeal before Charley and the others come across from the camp. Titch told you that his father doesn't want you or me to see whatever it is he and the other men are going to do over there, didn't he?"

"Yes."

"All right then," she said, "hurry up and get it done. And mind you, I really don't think that you or I should be looking at them when they do get over there."

"Yes, Mum."

She went down to the house and I across to the storeroom, to where it still stands, a solid stone structure, some fifty feet apart from the old house site, the first building ever to be built on Oonaderra. I got the bucket of oatmeal and took it over to Nellie.

When I came back to the house, after feeding the horse, I tiptoed into my father's office-cum-gunroom and found his binoculars. The window was open and looked directly out across the front veranda, so I had a commanding view of the camp on my left and the old house site on my right, without being seen myself. I pulled a chair to the window and sat down to watch and wait. I had the binoculars trained on the camp and there was movement going on around Tajalli's mia-mia, but I couldn't make out who was there or what they were doing because of the trees and high pandanus roots blocking my view.

I waited until I was almost on the verge of giving up. The suddenly a tall figure emerged, not through the trees around the camp, as I had expected, but through the palms on the beach. I swung the glasses on to him. It was Tajalli, naked, except for his lap-lap; his body was covered from head to feet in white horizontal lines—exactly as it had been on the night I had watched him from behind the tree when he had stood facing the assembled tribesmen in front of the blazing corroboree fires.

He stood there for a moment or two and then came striding from the beach toward the slope of the rise. In his right hand he was carrying his great shield, and in his left hand he was grasping a bundle of long hunting spears. The woven bag that I had first seen on the day I sneaked into his mia-mia was dangling from his wrist.

Halfway between the rise and the beach, at ap-

168

proximately the two-hundred-yard line of demarcation, he stopped and looked back at the camp. I swung the binoculars over there. The others who had been with him were nowhere to be seen. I turned the glasses back on to Tajalli. Every marking on him stood out in stark clarity, even to the whites of his fingernails against the black skin of his hands. He looked to left and right, as though he were afraid of the step he was about to take across the "line." Fear and strain showed in his eyes and in the taut clenching of his jaw.

Then he stepped over into the taboo area . . . and paused again.

I felt my heart pounding, as though I, too, faced his ordeal of braving the invisible power of Oona his god.

Then with unhesitating, long steps, he began to stride ahead in a long-legged, easy, graceful way.

I hastily withdrew from the window until he had passed on. Then I moved back to the other end of it to watch him as he approached the old site and stood before it, with his back to me, at the center of the double row of stump holes between which the dray had been pushed under the house.

He laid his shield and other things on the ground and, taking a spear, he walked between the center stump holes and began to drive the point of it down into the churned-up dust and debris lying there. When he had located what he was probing for, he drove the spear down hard into the ground and left it there.

He continued on with the other spears until he had four of them driven into the earth between the stump holes to form an enclosed oblong about eight feet long and six feet wide.

Next he took from the woven bag a length of looped cord wound around a bone. Through the binoculars, the ends of the bone appeared similar to the ends of the thigh bone of a native tiger cat, but I could not be really sure that that's what it was. Then he noosed the looped end of the cord on to one of the spear shafts and walked along unraveling the cord from the bone to the next spear, twisting it around the shaft until he had enclosed the ground inside the spears with a "fence" of the cord. He left the bone hanging from the end of the last spear he had tied.

All the while, he faced the sea. Then he knelt outside the fence and began to remove the earth from inside with his bare hands, scooping it from as far across the oblong as he could reach and filling it into the stump holes out of the way.

He went around the fence on his knees until he had cleared all the dust and debris away from what he was looking for. Even with the binoculars I couldn't see what it was he was unearthing.

He finished the task and went to where his things were lying on the ground. He took from the woven bag what looked like two dead birds, until I recognized them as the feathered "shoes" I had seen on the day I had entered his mia-mia. The "shoes" were, as I learned later, Kadiatcha shoes—kept, as many authorities believe, for the sole purpose of encircling a man's mia-mia if he has broken an important tribal law, to let him know that the ceremony of the Pointing of the Bone has been performed against him. When the victim sees the tracks of the shoes around his mia-mia, he knows that his spirit has been taken away and sent back to the Dreamtime, and he invariably wills himself to die. The tracks left by the shoes—because of their boat-shaped bottoms—leave no tell-tale evidence of where they commence or end, so the condemned man concludes that a debbil-debbil of witchcraft has encircled him, leaving no trail to or from his mia-mia. The man wearing the shoes is always very careful to brush away his tracks with a leafy branch as he backs away to a safe distance to take off the shoes and run away.

However, the Kadiatcha shoes that Tajalli was putting on were being used this time for a different purpose: the exorcizing of a debbil-debbil *away* from the old house site.

With the shoes on, Tajalli began to walk toward the cord-encircled enclosure in a peculiar to-and-fro rocking gait caused by the boat-shaped bottoms of the shoes. Then he slowly paced around the fence, firmly planting one shoe after the other in the soft ground until he had made their imprints right around the enclosure and was back to where he had started.

Then, looking behind him, he began to step from the enclosure, following the tracks he had made coming in; but after each backward step he paused, bent down, and brushed the earth with his hands, obliterating the imprint of his tracks right back to where his shield and bag lay.

He took off the shoes and left them lying on the ground while he returned to the fence with his bag and shield. This time he stepped under the cord into the enclosure and squatted in its center, facing the sea, with the bag in his left hand and his shield by his right side.

Although his back was to me, I could plainly see the left profile of his face through the binoculars. His lips were moving in some chant, but because of the distance and the sound of the breakers on the wind, I couldn't hear it.

He kept chanting for quite some time. Then suddenly he raised the bag and let its contents fall in front of him. He stared down at them, remaining motionless for perhaps three or four minutes in contemplation. Then he covered them with the shield.

That done, he stood up, turned toward the camp, and cupped his hands to his mouth. Clear and distinct on the wind I heard him give the "Woop, woop, woop, woop, w-o-o-o-o-p" call of the swamp pheasant.

I moved to the other side of the window and trained the glasses on the camp as three figures in lap-laps and painted white like Tajalli came running through the trees, one carrying the two shovels borrowed from me by Tajurra. I recognized the three as old Maratjira, Tobundi, and Trokka, tribal elders.

Just when I was getting set to see what would happen next, Mum called from the back of the house, "Jimmy! Jimmy! Where are you?"

I quickly replaced the binoculars, hurriedly tiptoed through the door on to the side veranda and over the rail. "Coming," I called to make it appear I was coming from the direction of the well. But I have a shrewd suspicion that she, too, had been watching Tajalli from the kitchen window.

In the kitchen she put her finger to her lips and said, "Listen."

I listened. In the living room Grandfather's clock began to strike eight o'clock in slow, measured whirrings of the hammer lifting and striking the gong.

"Mum!" I said. "How did you manage to get it going again?"

"I didn't do anything except turn the hands to the right time by my watch half an hour ago. Then I just gave the pendulum a swing and left it. I didn't even think it had started until I heard it whirring to strike the hour. I'm so glad it did, because I've suddenly got a feeling that . . . "

"Yes, Mum?" I asked, waiting to hear what the clock's striking had signified to her. But she just laughed and said, "Oh, nothing, dear. Let's forget it. Now how about getting some wood and water into the kitchen, or you won't be getting any lunch!"

"OK. Right away!"

In between fetching the wood and the water, and the other jobs she found for me to do, I managed enough time to watch what was going on over at the old site.

I missed what went on when the three elders reached the site and saw, as I presume Tajalli would show them, the contents of his bag lying inside the enclosure under his shield.

172

I saw that they were filling in the stump holes and leveling off the ground. They worked through the morning into the afternoon. Finally they carried up from the beach big chunks of coral and encircled the whole site with them.

When that was done, Tajalli wound the cord back onto the bone and replaced it in the bag, where I suppose he had put the Kadiatcha shoes because they were no longer on the ground. He gathered up the spears, the bag, and his shield, and they all left the site, Trokka carrying the shovels. My one thought was to go over and see what was in the hollow Tajalli had dug with his hands inside the enclosure.

But any illusions I had about taking the rest of the afternoon off were soon dispelled when my mother called me to come and help her plant her Dorothy Perkins rose by the back steps.

We were just finishing when Tajalli, now back in his khaki workclothes, appeared from around the side of the house carrying the two shovels.

" 'Lo, Missus. 'Lo, Jimmy."

His sudden appearance took Mum and me completely by surprise. It was the first time any of his tribe had come to the house in friendliness.

He smiled, put down the shovels, and said, "All bad thing go now, Missus; him finish altogether now. You want have look longa thing belonga Oona people over there?"

"You bet!" I answered before Mum could say, "Yes, Charley, thanks. We like see thing belonga your people."

We went across with him to the site and stood just outside the coral circle, looking at the place where he had worked alone that morning. And there, in the hollow he had dug, lay a long, shining black stone, totally unlike any other rock on Oonaderra. It was oval-shaped, and about six feet long and four feet wide in the center. Etched into its surface was Oona—the great turtle! Its outline had been chipped by human hands in the long, long ago and into the gouged-out replica of the turtle had been cemented shining mother of pearl. All around the turtle were geometric drawings, whorls, and signs, picked out in pearl shell and containing meaning which only the Aborigines understand.

My mother said. "It's beautiful, Charley, who do this fella thing? Who put that fella stone longa this place?"

Tajalli grinned. "Dunno, Missus. Father belonga me tell me, when me pickanninny, all about this fella stone fall down here long time before white people come." He pointed up to the sky to indicate where the stone, probably a meteorite, had come from.

I edged closer to the stone, but Mum restrained me and told me to keep outside the encircling coral. She said to Tajalli, "Me no know this fella stone under house. What for you no tell me, tell Mr. Brent?"

He answered, "Nobody ask me. Suppose I tell Mr. Brent, maybe he say me cheeky fella, get mad longa me."

Mum smiled at his surmisal of what Dad's reaction would no doubt have been, but behind her smile was still the grief she was unable to reconcile herself to. To change the subject, she said, "Rain stay away altogether too long now, Charley. Suppose rain no come soon, all the stock die."

"You no more worry, Missus!" he answered. "Me make rain come back longa Oonaderra quick smart! Have plenty grass, plenty water. All the cattle, all the horse get fat quick, like fat fella pig!"

Mum looked at him; I looked at him, thinking he must be joking. But Tajalli was quite serious about his ability to invoke the rain-god to send the rain we so desperately needed to get the grass growing. Mum said, "You speak truth, Charley?"

He nodded vigorously. "Too right, Missus! Me listen longa wind; him tell me listen longa mornin' when sun come up; maybe tell me light little fella fire quick smart, make rain come longa wind by and by."

"I hope that fella wind say it all right, Charley," she said. "You make rain come, I give you big fella ration, big fella bag longa lolly, longa 'bacca."

"All right, Missus, I do longa morning, when sun come up."

I chipped in and said, "Hey, why not give Tajalli a bit of a down payment on it now, eh? Couldn't we give him all those cakes and tarts left over from last night? Couldn't we?"

"Why, yes, of course! But we can do even better than that—he can come over and have a cup of tea and something to eat now. All right, Charley?"

Tajalli, totally unaccustomed to such an invitation, just smiled and nodded acceptance. But over at the house, no amount of coaxing could overcome his shyness about entering it. He excused himself by saying, "No like sit longa chair, longa table, Missus."

So he sat on the top step of the back veranda and had his cup of tea and cakes, with me beside him.

When he had finished, he thanked us and left without taking the parcel Mum had made up for him. I explained to her that it was not customary for him or any elders to do a woman's work of carrying food that had been cooked.

Later in the evening, the women came to collect their water. But now, safe from any fear of the debbil-debbil that had been exorcized from the house, they came crowding around the back steps to see into it for the first time, and, of course, to collect the big parcel which they lost no time in taking back to the camp with their water for the feast later on.

How strange it seemed to see the tribesmen making their way ceremoniously from the camp over to their ancient, sacred Bora Ring, talking and gesturing excitedly about its return to them and all that it meant to their belief in Oona, the great turtle god.

For me there was one disappointment: I had hoped Tajurra would come to the house, but he didn't.

Next morning, in my eagerness to see once more the ceremony of Tajalli's rain making, I was waiting in my room when the rim of the sun rose above the horizon. As I watched its reflection stain the sea and the sky in a flaring blood-red glow, I saw Tajalli and Tajurra walk out in their lap-laps through the pandanus palms onto the beach where they stood like ebony statues against the glow of the sunrise. Then they walked back and disappeared behind the high pandanus roots.

I raced over. They were kneeling on the ground beneath the palms.

" 'Lo, there," I greeted them.

" 'Lo, Jimmy," Tajurra answered, but not Tajalli. He was too intent on watching the stick with its little pennant of limp red flannel. A small mound of dried mangrove leaves sat in front of the leader. The piece of milky pine, a tuft of dried swamp reed, the firestick, and his woven bag were all in readiness. I sat down to watch Tajalli. I glanced at Tajurra. He seemed to be on the point of laughing, which was indeed a strange thing under the circumstances.

After sitting in silence for quite a while, the morning breeze sprang up to toss the little pennant anywhere but in the direction Tajalli was waiting for. This went on for some time. Then he suddenly sucked in his breath; the breeze had swung to the northeast, coming in steadily now from out over the Coral Sea. With a whispered "Tirjila! Tirjila! Tirjila!" Tajalli began twirling the firestick in the hole in the piece of milky pine, with the tuft of dried swamp reed alongside it, until the point of the stick sparked and the reed caught and began to smolder. Tajalli grabbed up the tuft in his cupped hands, blew it alight, and thrust it under the little heap of leaves, which burst into purple and orange flames and was consumed in a flash, leaving only white ash.

Next Tajalli carefully shaped the ash into the outline of a turtle. Then he took the bag and tipped its contents out between his knees to reveal the "cat's-eyes," the teji stones, the bandicoot's skull, the dried lizards, and the tiny mummified baby turtle: a haphazard arrangement which Tajalli apparently recognized as favorable omens, because he uttered a soft "Wah!" of approval and said, with quiet conviction, "Ah! Rain come now longa this place by and by soon."

"When?" I asked.

He shrugged. "Maybe two day, maybe three day. By and by bird talk all about rain come; frog talk about rain come; by and by everything talk longa Oonaderra, say good fella rain come longa this place."

While Tajalli was gathering up his things, Tajurra winked at me to get up and follow him. He and I walked around to the creek bed where he said, "I know rain come all same, Tajalli."

"How?" I asked.

He pointed to a line of ants, emerging from a hole low down in the creek bank and traveling up to high ground, and said, "That fella ant know all about rain come, Jimmy; him clear out, run away quick smart."

"What for he do that?" I asked.

"Him no want stop longa that fella hole when water come down longa creek, when rain come."

Which was as good a natural explanation as any, I suppose, on which to base a weather forecast. He then pointed up at the branches of the she-oak above us and said, "Little fella white thing longa tree know rain come, like ant know."

He was pointing up at the tree's branches dotted with tiny white exudations made by gall-wasp larvae when the tree's sap is due to start flowing with the approach of good rain.

I was satisfied that Tajurra, like his father, had read the natural signs that rain was on the way to Oonaderra at last. And I suspect now that shrewd old

Tajalli had been fully aware, on both occasions when I had seen him perform the rain-making ceremony, that rain *was* on the way before he would risk his reputation with a forecast.

I laughed and changed the subject to ask, "Why you no come longa house, Tajurra, when men go home?"

He shrugged and answered, "Me tell Tajalli me like go longa house, eat tucker longa you; him say me altogether bad cheeky fella boy; tell me no more go longa house, eat tucker. Him say, maybe by and by mother belonga you tell me sit longa step, eat tucker. Maybe by and by, eh?"

I guessed that Tajalli had imagined his son might be trying to impose on my mother, and he probably also thought that Tajurra would not conduct himself properly. So I said, "You no cheeky fella, Tajurra. You like have breakfast longa me now, eh?"

He nodded eagerly.

"All right," I said. "I ask Tajalli let you come longa house."

Tajalli had walked down to the water's edge and was gazing out over the Coral Sea. We went down to him, and I explained that Tajurra was welcome to come and have breakfast with Mum and me, if he were allowed.

Tajalli thought for a moment or two, then said, "All right, Jimmy. Suppose he no more cheeky boy longa house, he go, when he get clothes on."

I thanked him and hurried over to the house to prepare Mum for Tajurra's arrival. She was in the kitchen getting breakfast. She smiled when I told her and said, "Well it's just as well we're having curry and rice—he can eat that with a spoon instead of being embarrassed trying to use a knife and fork."

And so Tajurra came over, dressed in his boots, khaki, shirts, pants, and hat. I met him at the back steps. He was shy until Mum called out, "Come on, you two, before this food gets cold." He dropped his hat on the veranda and followed me in—the first Aborigine ever to cross the threshold into the house of the Brents, and to sit with us that Sunday morning at breakfast.

Just as Tajalli had predicted, on the morning of the second day after his weather forecast, the storm birds began their incessant calls warning of storms and rain approaching Oonaderra.

On the radio that afternoon the weather report also confirmed, "A stream of moist air over the Coral Sea is approaching Cape York Peninsula, with storms and heavy rain likely over the next few days. . . . "

By nightfall the sky and the sea had merged into one great blackness broken only by flashes of lightning. And the frogs—millions of them!—began their raucous calls of "Quart pot! Quart pot!" around the lagoon and along the creek banks, in welcome to the rain that was already beginning to spit and drum on the roof. I got into bed and lay there listening to the boom of thunder above the clamor of the frogs, the sound of the rain and all the creatures of the night in a full chorus of gratitude for Oonaderra's deliverance from the drought.

The last thing I remember before I fell asleep was my grandfather's clock striking midnight.

Glossary

barata: a secret, poisonous substance once used by Aborigines for mercy killings, which is untraceable in the body.

beeli sticks: polished, rounded hardwood sticks beaten together and used in tribal corroborees.

billabong: usually a small pond filled by a connecting channel from a stream or river when heavy rain causes the water level to rise; when the rain stops and the water level falls, the water in the billabong remains.

billy: a billy-can—the Australian bushman's teapot. A can with a lid, and a wire handle (bucket style) for carrying it.

bogey: a word used by white Australian bushmen to mean taking a bath in a creek, river or waterhole.

"bone-pointing": This was practiced by many Aboriginal tribes. A man wishing to use a "pointing bone" would go into the bush, place the bone in the ground, and repeat curses over it. During the night it would be

180

pointed at the victim, and magic chants sung over it. The victim would invariably sicken and die.

boongs and *burries*: contemptuous words used by white people for the Aborigines.

Bora Ring: a sacred circle usually enclosing a revered object, such as a rock or a group of rocks. After initiation, the young men are allowed to step within the circle to have the tribal secrets revealed to them. It is taboo ground to everyone else.

bullroarer: a carved flat piece of wood that varies in length from six to twenty-four inches—the average being about twelve inches long and three inches wide. It is usually incised on both surfaces with symbols—circles, wavy lines, U-shapes, and lines. The bullroarer is held by a long human-hair cord tied through a hole at its top and whirled around the head, making a distinctive sound which is recognized by all as a sign that a ceremony is in progress.

coolamons: These serve as dishes and for carrying items of food such as yams, fruits, shellfish, etc. The Aboriginal women seek out trees with large "elbow" branches and cut out the bark around the elbow to make the oblong coolamons they want.

corroboree: Among the Oonas, there are different forms of this ceremony. One entails the participation of the whole tribe—like a play—in which tribal lore and the prowess of the hunters are retold in song and mimicry for the education of the young. The other corroborees are attended only by men; they are held for the initiation of boys into manhood, and for those purposes for which tribal lore demands a full congress of men, when the leader and elders report on the guardianship of the tribe's affairs and decisions concerning the welfare of the tribe are made.

didgeridu: a wooden wind instrument similar to an alpenhorn.

digger: This word came into wide usage in World War I to describe the Australian soldiers who came to be known by that name. It probably originated in the vernacular used by the miners on the gold fields in the early days of the alluvial gold rushes of Australia—hence the Australian term "the Diggers."

dillybag: a woven string bag used by Aboriginal women as a carryall from camp to camp.

Dreamtime: The Dreamtime or Creation period was when the Aboriginal world was formed. The Aborigines believe that all creatures once lived below the flat surface of the land. At a precise time in history they broke through the flat plain and began life on earth. The activities of those legendary heroes, who made the landscape features and created the Aboriginal world, are perpetuated in song and ritual. The Aborigines believe in an afterlife, and that when they die their spirit returns to the Dreamtime.

dugong: the manatee, or sea cow, so called because its muzzle resembles that of a cow. It is a large mammal inhabiting the waters of the Great Barrier Reef; it grazes on seaweed and sea grass.

gins: A disrespectful word used by careless white people to describe the Aboriginal women.

goanna: an Australian word meaning iguana. There are several species of goanna, ranging from the smaller water goannas up to the large tree-climbing species.

honey ants: These ants establish a nest, or colony, deep under ground. They then begin a storage vault in the nest by selected ants suspending themselves by their mandibles from roots on the ceiling of the vault. The worker ants then collect and bring nectar to the nest, which the storage ants accept and store in their distensible stomachs for the colony to use when required.

Kadiatcha shoes: Certain tribes believed that a death was invariably due to the evil magical influences of some enemy. When the guilt was fixed upon a particular person, either a man called Kadiatcha was chosen to avenge the death, or an individual would go forth on his own initiative wearing the shoes, which were made from blood, feathers, and human-hair string and rounded at each end so as to make it impossible to distinguish from which direction the footprints came. The man whose mia-mia was encircled by the prints of the Kadiatcha shoes knew that the bone had been "pointed" at him and invariably willed himself to die.

lap-lap: a loin cloth once worn by most Aboriginal men and women living in tribal communities before the white man and missionaries introduced the clothing of civilization. These lap-laps were woven from bark fiber to form dangling skirts suspended from a bark belt. Tied around the waist, they made short skirts to maintain the tribal laws of adult respectability enforced by tribal elders.

lolly: an Australian abbreviation of lollipop, meaning sweets or candy.

mia-mia: a thatched, beehive-shaped dwelling made of blady grass and pandanus leaves which individual families of a tribe use when they stay in a camp for a long while.

Miaja Kadi: the Oona tribe's incantation to the spirit of a murdered leader.

mullee grub: the larva of a large rain-forest beetle which feeds on rotting timber on the forest floor.

myall: an Aboriginal word used to describe Aborigines who have had no contact with civilization.

Myee Wundul: the Oona Tribe's incantation to the spirit of a murdered wife of a leader.

nulla-nulla: a wooden club.

Palm Island: a mission settlement off Townsville on the North Queensland Coast.

plurry: a slang word evolved from "bloody" and used by both black and white Australians.

pufftaloons: a dough made from self-raising flour into scones and then fried (preferably) in bacon grease.

purra shell: a brilliantly banded seashell, similar in shape to but larger than a periwinkle, used by some coastal tribes in the barata ceremony.

scrubber: a wild bull that has eluded roundups.

station: a large Australian sheep or cattle property.

teji stones: unusual pieces of quartz with various colors in layers and worn smooth by the action of the sea. Some tribes prize these stones as sacred objects from the Dreamtime.

trepang: an edible sea slug found in North Queensland coastal waters; the Chinese cure it and consider it a great delicacy.

trevalli: a large, tasty fish fairly plentiful in the Great Barrier Reef waters.

waitawhile: a rain-forest plant of long canes (lawyer canes) with a secondary growth of whiplash canes armed with vicious curved hooks to catch the unwary traveler on horseback.

Walkabout: The Oona Aborigines go Walkabout usually for the duration of the Wet. They leave their settled camp to go in search of different food to supplement their diet, for example, water birds' eggs and lily buds. The Walkabout is also a bartering trip between tribes, and a time when young initiated men and women of compatible tribes are exchanged.

The Wet and the Dry: The Wet usually, but not always, lasts from about the beginning of January to the middle of April; and the Dry usually extends from about April until the end of the year. Occasional rain falls in the Dry.

woomera: a length of grooved hardwood about eighteen inches long with a peg fixed at one end to take the butt of a spear. Two pieces of bailer shell are fixed on the other end to form a handle. The woomera extends the length of the arm, making it possible to propel the spear with great force.

yabbies: freshwater crayfish. They resemble small lobsters and grow to about six inches in length.

yakka: hard work—from a local Queensland Aboriginal dialect.

yarrabah: a North Queensland mission station.